HIS SECRET DAUGHTER

EMMA BENNET

Published 2014 by Joffe Books, London

www.joffebooks.com

This book is a work of fiction. Names, characters, businesses, organizations, places and events are either the product of the author's imagination or are used fictitiously. Any resemblance to actual persons, living or dead, events or locales is entirely coincidental. The spelling is British English.

ISBN 978 1503203792

DEDICATION

To my fabulous Nan, the most glamorous woman I've ever met in real life.

CONTENTS

Chapter 1

Iris Brown strolled contentedly and unhurriedly along the leafy avenue, her young daughter happy in her stroller. Though her small frame struggled pushing the heavy buggy up the slope towards the park café and her child's promised ice-cream, Iris delighted in the glorious feeling of the late afternoon sunshine warming her back against the chill of the spring breeze. If she really concentrated on the beautiful blue sky and greenery surrounding her, she could almost imagine she wasn't actually in the centre of London.

Taking her time, and making the most of the fresh air after being sat at her laptop working for the last few hours, Iris chatted away to her daughter, asking about her day at playgroup and what she'd like for tea.

Iris was so enjoying her walk that at first she was unaware of the group of very serious and intense businessmen striding along the gravel path towards them. Only when they were about to pass did Iris fleetingly register them, noting their dark hair and tanned skins. But hearing a curt "buono" in a voice she instantly recognised, she experienced a sickening jolt throughout her body and became rooted to the ground with shock.

It couldn't be. It just couldn't be. She caught the eye of the speaker and saw recognition reflected there. He stood stock still, looking as astonished as she felt.

Surprised as she was, Iris couldn't help but notice that Sergio Batista-Sanchez was just as handsome as ever. His confident, faintly haughty air hadn't changed a bit in the three years since she'd last seen him. Tall and imposing, he was the very image of the impeccably dressed, conservative man of business. Only his ever-so-slightly too long and messy hair hinted that there might be an undercurrent of rebellion hidden beneath the surface.

With horror, Iris tracked Sergio's eyes as they moved from her to her daughter and took in her beautiful Mediterranean complexion which contrasted starkly with Iris's own far paler skin and blond hair. Understanding flashed across his dark eyes, and he took a hesitant step towards them.

Impulsively, Iris fled, her heart thumping wildly in her chest as she sought to quell the terror she could feel rapidly building inside. There was little if any thought involved in her actions other than her desperate need to get away from Sergio as quickly as possible. She hadn't gone to so much trouble just to have it all ruined now. Trying to quell her panic, she put her head down and concentrated on getting to the relative safety of her home. She knew Sergio would be watching her go, and taking note of the direction she took, but was also sure he wasn't the sort to run after her. That would be far too undignified for such an important man in front of his not-quite-so-important colleagues.

She reached the sanctuary of their poky rented ground-floor flat and locked the door firmly behind her. Her heart rate began to slow, and she was able to deal with her little girl's continued requests for ice cream.

She found a choc ice in the depths of the freezer, placating her easy-going daughter. Iris's mind returned to the problem of what she should do.

Would leaving London help? Probably not: she was sure now Sergio knew about her secret, he would follow her wherever she went. He was the type of man who could find out anything he wanted with just one phone call. Maybe she could buy herself some time if she went to her mother's? It wouldn't take long to throw some things in a bag, and her mother was only about an hour away by train. But how would her mother react? They weren't close, hadn't seen each other for well over a year, and her mother was a woman who liked her whole life to be very carefully organised, with absolutely no surprises. Children were never a welcome addition to her schedule. Iris was still thinking about calling to test the waters, when she heard her front-door buzzer. She had to admit she was impressed with his speed. How had her ex-lover managed to get rid of his work associates, find out her address, and be outside her front door in less than half an hour?

Iris's immediate reaction was to ignore him, but the buzzer continued relentlessly, and she finally went over to the door, telling her little girl to stay where she was in the kitchen. Steeling herself, and taking a deep breath in an effort to control her nerves, she opened the door. She managed to appear perfectly calm and composed to a furious Sergio who tried to step into the flat saying: "Iris. We need to talk. Now."

She blocked his way. "I don't have anything to say to you."

"I think you do."

"You can't just turn up on my doorstep making demands; I don't work for you anymore."

"You can either talk to me now or to my lawyer, your choice," he replied sharply.

Iris had a sudden vision of Sergio's lawyer, a vicious little man, notorious for using whatever ruthless tactics necessary to win a case. She really didn't fancy her chances up against him.

"What do you want to know?" she asked.

"What is her name?" he said, his dark eyes peering beyond Iris, clearly looking for her daughter.

"Paola."

Sergio turned his gaze to Iris, searching her face.

"A very beautiful name. And very Spanish," he said with a raised eyebrow.

When this received no response, he continued, "Why didn't you tell me I had a daughter?"

She hesitated, debating whether to deny his paternity.

Sergio, sensing her thoughts, quickly said, "Don't lie to me, it's obvious."

"You'd better come in," she conceded, realising she should be counting her blessings that he hadn't had time to drag his solicitor along with him.

He strode into the narrow hall and followed her through the sitting room and into the cramped kitchen.

"Would you like a cup of tea?" she asked, regretting the offer as soon as she'd made it. She couldn't possibly sit down and drink tea with this man: she needed him out of her home, and ideally out of her life again, as soon as humanly possible.

"No, this won't take long," he said distractedly, looking at the small wooden table at the far end of the room, where Paola was contentedly working her way through her choc ice. All three were silent as father and daughter surveyed each other, both of them hesitant to move towards the other. However, Paola appeared to realise he was someone significant.

"Hello!" she said, smiling and cheerfully waving her spoon.

"Hello," Sergio reiterated cautiously, shaking his head, as if waking from a trance. He returned his attention to Iris, "I have contacted my lawyers. We can go through the formality of a paternity test if you wish, but I really see no need: she's my daughter. We can do this the easy way or the hard way. I am at a conference in Geneva for the next few days but I return Friday night. I shall expect you and Paola at my house on Saturday at two p.m."

"What if we're not available on Saturday at two?" Iris asked petulantly.

"Then I shall begin legal proceedings for full custody," he replied, not missing a beat.

"You're certainly very organised for someone who only found out he was a father less than an hour ago."

"So you admit she is mine."

"Yes," she said softly.

"Then we have nothing more to discuss. I shall see you both on Saturday." He turned to his daughter and added, "Goodbye Paola," in a gentler tone of voice.

"Bye-bye," Paola replied cheerfully, licking chocolate off her fingers.

Sergio took one long, last look at his daughter and left with a gruff declaration of "I shall let myself out."

* * *

It was much later on, after Paola had been put to bed, that Iris had a chance to properly digest the afternoon's momentous events. She poured a glass of wine and prepared some pasta for supper and her mind went over and over that chance meeting in the park. Oh, how she wished she'd taken a different route home! Then none of this would be happening and she and Paola would be free to carry on with their lives as they pleased.

She settled down to watch some television and her mind wandered to her affair with Sergio. She remembered her first day as Sergio's assistant; it was her first job out of university and she'd been amazed they'd hired her. Sergio hadn't been at either of her two interviews, and she was looking forward to meeting the man whom she'd already heard a great deal about.

Iris had taken extra-special care over her appearance that morning, getting up early to ensure she wouldn't have to rush. On seeing Sergio she'd been glad she'd made the effort. When they met in a crowded corridor everything else had seemed to vanish as they stared, mesmerised by each other.

He was certainly older than she was by a good few years, she'd guessed he was in his early-thirties. He was obviously very self-assured, though there was that moment, as they'd first locked eyes, when his cool demeanour had faltered. He'd appeared momentarily dazed. As he'd recovered himself, a small smile had played on his lips.

Sergio was Iris's opposite: tall and dark to her small and fair. Slightly stern until he smiled, and then his whole face opened up. She'd suspected he had a very different side underneath his tough manner.

He'd strode over and they'd been introduced. Iris had known he was Spanish, so his accent should have come as no surprise, but his deep, manly voice, combined with the sexy, foreign lilt to his speech, had taken her breath away. Somehow she'd known her life would never be the same again.

Sergio had been a good boss, treating his employees fairly. But he'd also expected them to work very hard. It had been after a particularly long meeting which had gone on until almost nine in the evening, that Iris had found out for certain that her interest in Sergio was reciprocated.

The two of them were the only people left in the conference room. Sergio rubbed his tired face and closed his laptop with an air of finality. His gaze locked on Iris, and he gave her a slow, languid smile.

"Would you like to join me for dinner?" he'd asked, as if it were the most natural thing in the world. She'd suspected that agreeing to his invitation was probably not the most sensible choice, but had been unable to stop herself.

Before she could think what was happening, Iris had found herself sitting across from Sergio at a table in a very nice restaurant five minutes' walk from their offices. As they'd talked and joked, she'd realised that as well as being very attracted to this man, she also really liked him and was thoroughly enjoying his company.

Nothing romantic had happened between them that night. Sergio had been a perfect gentleman, even insisting upon paying for a taxi to take her home safely. She might have said yes to continuing the evening at his place. His pull on her was magnetic.

Over the next couple of months, dinner or post-work drinks had become a regular occurrence. Iris had loved spending these evenings with Sergio, and had grown more and more comfortable around him. At the same time, the sexual tension had been amazing: Iris had been practically shaking with longing every moment she was with him. His dark eyes were so intense they'd felt as if they were boring into her soul.

At last the evening arrived when Sergio made his move. As they left an Italian restaurant, he had kissed her passionately on the lips. A kiss that had promised much more. She'd followed him to the taxi and he'd climbed in next to her and given directions to his house.

That night with Sergio had been perfect, surpassing Iris's every fantasy. For the first time in her life she'd felt completely and totally in love. However, despite Sergio's attempts to convince her not to leave the following morning, she'd known the office busybodies would have a lot to say if they saw her not only arriving with her boss, but also wearing her clothes from the day before. After a last kiss, she'd turned down Sergio's offer to call his car for her, and had slipped out of the front door. She'd walked to the main road, caught a bus home, showered and changed, and arrived at work by nine.

Floating on a cloud of happiness, Iris had settled down to work, hoping that Sergio might have sent her an email. Maybe he'd even send her some flowers, although part of her had hoped he wouldn't do that, she hadn't been ready for the gossipmongers to get hold of her secret just yet.

She'd checked her inbox every few minutes, but nothing from Sergio had arrived and she'd been forced to admit to herself that it was very, very unlikely that Sergio was the type to send a romantic message over the office email system. Resolving to concentrate on work, she'd pushed her new lover to the back of her mind and had managed to focus pretty well for a while at least. But then with lunchtime approaching, not only had he not called or emailed, but, quite unusually, Iris hadn't seen him at all. His office was locked and dark. Checking Sergio's diary, she'd confirmed that all his appointments had been cancelled. As the changes hadn't been made by her, they must have been organised before she'd come in that morning.

Troubled, but unsure whether she truly had reason to be, Iris had picked up her bag and decided to get some fresh air. Stopping off at the ladies on the way, she'd just locked the cubicle door when she heard footsteps and voices as two other women entered the bathroom.

"He just can't seem to help himself, can he?" one of the women had said, as Iris heard her rustling in her handbag.

"Well, can you blame him? He's a hot-blooded Spaniard, and these girls will keep throwing themselves at him. I don't think many men would refuse," the other said.

Iris's ears had pricked up at the mention of the word 'Spaniard' — were these women talking about her and Sergio, and if so how had they found out? And how dare they claim she threw herself at him!

"Whoever this latest one is, she's getting quite a bit of his attention. He called earlier and asked me to clear his diary of absolutely everything for the next week."

She'd had to fight to keep her balance when she heard this — the rat must have been arranging to meet another woman while his bed was still warm from her! And yet some of the things he'd said only hours earlier had led her to believe that he really had feelings for her. He'd seemed genuine. What an idiot she was: he was obviously just saying exactly what he'd known she wanted to hear. And she'd fallen for it hook, line, and sinker.

"Doesn't he usually keep his fun for the evenings and weekends?"

"Yes, normally it's business first for Mr Batista-Sanchez. Maybe this one's special?"

"Aren't they all, until he gets bored with them. I give it a fortnight," the second woman had replied with a laugh. "Come on, let's get some lunch, I'm starving."

Iris had managed to hold her emotions in check until both women had left, but then the hurt overwhelmed her and the tears began to flow freely. It had taken her several minutes to get them under control, but eventually she had. Then she tried to get matters clear in her mind: she and Sergio had had an amazing night together, but he hadn't promised her anything. Although he hadn't spoken of other women, he also hadn't said there weren't any, and as handsome, charming, and obviously wealthy as he was, he was bound to have plenty of female admirers. Should she really be surprised he'd go off with someone else just hours after taking her to bed? The biggest, and to Iris, most condemning piece of evidence, was Sergio booking several days off work: he'd certainly been energetic and healthy enough the night before. If he'd had some other good reason for not being at work, and wanted to see her again, he would have told her before she'd left his house.

She'd been made a fool of, but she wasn't going to let it happen again. Fixing her make-up in the bathroom mirror and ensuring no trace of her tears remained, she'd marched straight out of the building, resolved never to return. She certainly hadn't been prepared to give Sergio the satisfaction of seeing how humiliated she felt.

Her determination had only been strengthened a few weeks later when she'd stared at the two red lines showing up starkly on the white strip of the pregnancy test. A man like that would have no interest in a baby, and she would not let her child be rejected as coldly and heartlessly as she'd been. Anyway, Iris's pride simply wouldn't allow her to contact Sergio and tell him that she was having his baby: he would have assumed she was after his money, when nothing could be further from the case. All she'd ever wanted was his love.

Chapter 2

Iris thought all the feelings she'd had for Sergio had been carefully locked away in a tiny corner of her heart from where they'd never be accessed again. This had been essential, she knew, both for herself and for her daughter. So as she and Paola approached the black, imposing front door of Sergio's house on Saturday afternoon at two p.m., as demanded, Iris was frankly unprepared for the barrage of pain she experienced. As she steeled herself to knock, she felt like the breath had been knocked out of her. A whole cacophony of emotions threatened to engulf her — pain at how Sergio had hurt her, fear as to what he would do now he knew about Paola, and, strangely, the bitter-sweet recollection of the wonderful night she'd spent inside this very place, wrapped in Sergio's strong arms.

Despite only having been there once, Iris could not only recall its address perfectly (although she hated that Sergio had assumed she'd remember where it was), but its exterior and the rooms she'd been in.

Iris glanced down at her daughter sitting quietly in her pushchair. She made a final check that Paola really looked her best. Iris wanted him to see not only how beautiful their child was, but also how well cared for. She'd dressed

Paola just before they left, and they'd taken a taxi so there'd been very little opportunity for the busy two-year-old to dirty her pretty outfit or tangle her long, gleaming hair. Iris, on the other hand, had been ready for hours, her stomach in knots, wondering what demands Sergio would make and trying to reassure herself that he didn't really seem the sort to want to "play Daddy" for long. He'd soon get tired of his new "toy".

Sergio opened the door as she reached for the brass knocker. He'd obviously been watching out for them.

"Well, don't you look lovely, chiquita," said Sergio gently.

Iris began to extract her daughter from her pushchair. The combination of wiggly toddler and dodgy clasp made this task a lot harder than it should have been. Left with a sore thumb and flushed, embarrassed cheeks, Iris was finally able to get her daughter out. Paola walked happily over to Sergio and he took her outstretched hand.

"Would you like some help with that?" asked Sergio, indicating the buggy Iris was now fighting to fold up.

"I'm fine," she answered shortly, wishing he'd stop staring at her. She was sure her hands would work much better and the stupid contraption would be far more willing to close, without his eyes boring down upon her. The temperamental old thing always chose the worst moments to jam. Sergio and Paola politely waited for Iris to come into the house with them.

Finally accepting defeat, Iris muttered, "Actually, would you mind if I just left the pushchair up, in your hallway?"

"Not at all," he said, gesturing for her to follow him inside.

They went into his glamorous entrance hall, where Iris's grotty old pushchair looked extremely out of place. They continued into a large sitting room with stark white walls and an enormous marble fireplace, which, judging by the extremely clean grating, was never used. The heavy drapes at the windows were ridiculously opulent, yet, despite his obvious wealth, somehow Iris couldn't imagine the Sergio she knew buying them. They seemed too fussy for a man like him.

A mountain of toys filled one corner of the room, and Paola let out a giggle of delight and tottered over to investigate the treasures.

"That's completely unnecessary," Iris said.

"I thought she'd like something to play with," Sergio said with an edge to his voice, like he could tell she was close to becoming awkward and was giving her a warning.

She chose to ignore it and retorted: "I buy her plenty of toys." She was annoyed because she knew deep down there was no way she could afford to get her daughter even a quarter of what was piled up here.

"I am sure you do," he replied.

They glowered at each other.

"I shall have them sent to your home," he said, as though the matter was now closed.

"I've got no space for all these."

"Fine," he replied crossly. "They can stay here for when she visits."

The glares continued. Both of them were determined not to back down and break eye contact.

Finally, Paola's laughter distracted them as she attempted to use her toddler mountaineering skills to reach the peak of the toy pile. They rushed over to prevent the inevitable fall. Sergio reached her first, but stopped himself from grabbing his daughter, allowing Iris to help her down.

* * *

The visit went very slowly. Iris was on constant tenterhooks in case Paola broke one of the many very delicate and valuable-looking objects in Sergio's house. Thankfully her daughter was happily occupied with all the new goodies, and the best new toy of all: Sergio. She sat on his knee and gazed adoringly up at him as he asked Iris question after question about their child. He seemed pleasant enough, now, while Paola was with them, but Iris dreaded being alone with him. He must want answers as to why she'd kept his daughter a secret, and was probably waiting until Paola wasn't around to interrogate her. She knew that explaining would dredge up those memories she'd tried so hard to suppress.

Finally, at five, Iris felt they'd stayed long enough for her to be able to politely leave. "Paola will be needing her tea," she explained.

"She can eat here," he replied, looking at Paola for her approval. The little girl just wandered happily off to climb in a cardboard box.

"I don't think she'd eat the sort of food you have in," Iris said.

"Do you want to come and see what we've got for your tea, Paola? What's your favourite food?" he said.

"Biscuits!" Paola said cheerfully and abandoned her game to take her father's hand.

Sergio led the way into his vast, gleaming kitchen, full of various chrome appliances. When Sergio opened his large Sub-Zero fridge-freezer, there was plenty Iris recognised — it was toddler food heaven: fish fingers, chicken nuggets, and pizza vied for space with waffles, chips, cheese, grapes, strawberries, and little pot of fromage frais. It looked as if Sergio had read some sort of guide to what two-year-olds eat, and bought the lot.

"Wow," was all Iris could find to say. "You certainly went to a lot of trouble."

"I wasn't sure what she'd like, so I sent my housekeeper out to get a bit of everything."

Ah, the housekeeper, that figures, Iris thought. Of course he wouldn't actually bother to go to the supermarket himself. "Pasta's her favourite usually, but she's not that fussy," she replied.

Almost as if on cue, an attractive young woman, the quintessential English rose, with the sort of long, swishy hair Iris had always dreamed of having, came into the kitchen. She wore tight dark jeans, a vest top and high heels, and exuded an air of confidence Iris knew she herself would never achieve. She couldn't have been much older than her early twenties, and clearly felt at home here, which Iris most certainly did not.

"Serena, there you are," said Sergio with a friendly smile. "It is nearing my daughter's tea time. Could you possibly make her some pasta?"

"Of course, perhaps she'd like it with pesto?"

Sergio looked to Iris to confirm if this was okay, and she nodded.

"Shall I make her a side salad?" asked Serena in all seriousness.

"She's two," Iris replied. It came out snappier than she'd intended.

Sergio glared at Iris, and turned to Serena, "No, thank you."

Leaving Serena to get on with the cooking, they went back to the sitting room. Iris was beginning to feel trapped: she'd had enough now and wanted to go home, not wait around while some glamorous model-wannabe made pasta for her daughter.

Paola was oblivious to the tension and played happily. Sergio pushed her around the room on a trike. Iris felt redundant and almost an outsider, observing the happy scene.

All she wanted was to scoop her little girl up and take her back to the security of their flat. Away from Sergio, she would be able to breathe and untangle the afternoon's knotted web of emotions.

But despite her misgivings, Iris couldn't be so rude as to leave while someone was in the middle of making tea for Paola, nor did she want to risk Sergio's anger by doing so. He was a very powerful man, and he was right to assume she didn't want to come up against him. Not that there was any doubt in her mind that she'd fight Sergio with everything she had if he ever tried to take her daughter away from her. But she was prepared to play nicely with him, for now.

It wasn't long before Paola was called back to the kitchen for her tea. Thankfully, Serena disappeared as soon as Paola was settled at the table — Iris couldn't help feeling slightly inferior next to such a dazzling creature. She watched Sergio as Serena left the room, wanting to see if his eyes followed Serena's body as she went, but he appeared, for the moment at least, to be totally focussed on his daughter.

Paola loved Serena's homemade pesto sauce — Iris was torn between being proud of her for eating so well, and put out that she obviously preferred it to her mother's version, from a jar.

The second Paola put the last piece of penne into her mouth, Iris declared that they really had to go. With her bag and Paola's cardigan already collected, she pounced with a wet wipe and quickly cleaned up Paola's pesto-covered face. She was so fast neither the little girl nor Sergio had much of a chance to protest, before Paola was strapped into her buggy, and they were out of his house.

"I'll be in touch," Sergio said ominously as he closed the door behind them.

Despite his parting words, Iris certainly felt freer as she pushed her very tired toddler the short distance to the bus stop, finances wouldn't stretch to a second taxi. Gazing out of the bus window with a sleeping Paola on her lap, she allowed her mind to wander. On the positive side, the afternoon had gone better than it might have done. Sergio had been pleasant, and he and Paola had clearly enjoyed themselves together. In fact, the more she thought about the afternoon the happier she began to feel — the deep void of unease in her stomach hadn't gone, but she was confident Sergio wasn't the type to play daddy for long. Yes, he'd bought all those toys and filled his fridge with food for her, but that was the work of his housekeeper. It's not like he'd gone out and shopped for his daughter himself! Hopefully a few more afternoons like this would be more than enough for him to get any paternal impulses out of his system. Iris suspected that by the time he was back at the office on Monday, and all focused on making himself even more money, Paola's importance would start to diminish.

She manoeuvred the buggy off the bus, across the street, and up the awkward steps to her flat. She found herself comparing it to Sergio's house. She took in the flaking paint and the broken knocker as she performed the special jiggle with her keys necessary to open the door. It had been raining recently and the wood was swollen, so the jiggling had to be accompanied by a hefty shoulder barge.

Inside, Iris helped her daughter out of the pushchair, tentatively checking Paola's expression for any sign that she found her home lacking now she'd experienced her father's fancier residence. Paola seemed as cheerful as ever though, toddling around, piling more and more toys into the bubble bath Iris ran for her.

After Paola had had her fill of stories and was safely tucked up in bed, Iris poured herself a glass of wine and put on a DVD. Emotionally drained, and more than a little insecure, she tried to focus on the positives: the afternoon had gone as well as possible, and was over. Nothing particularly terrible had happened: Sergio had been polite, and hopefully it was only a matter of time before this fad of his had run its course.

She had to admit he had been very good with Paola. He was patient and had seemed genuinely interested in her. But then it's easy to be those things when you only have to carry it off for a few hours.

Needing reassurance, she concentrated on the hope that once the novelty had worn off, she and Paola would be able to get back to normal again.

* * *

The following morning, the hum from the stirring traffic outside her bedroom window pulled Iris from deep sleep. Warm and happy, she stretched, sleepily grasping for the receding remnants of her disturbed dream. But dismay swiftly replaced contentment as the recollection of Sergio and his masculine, toned body swam into focus.

After she'd discovered she was pregnant, and had broken contact with Sergio, he'd frequently haunted her dreams. But she'd somehow managed to quell her unconscious, and hadn't fantasised about him for well over a year.

This new dream wasn't like the old ones though — they usually entailed the repetition of their wonderful night together. In this one they'd been on a beach: Sergio had kissed her; a soft, slightly lingering brush of the lips, before they'd pulled apart to help Paola finish her sandcastle. It was a perfect family moment. Just a shame it would never actually happen, thought Iris, surprised she'd come up with such a thing at all. She'd been certain any romantic feelings she'd had for Sergio had been well and truly buried. But then maybe you can never fully extinguish passion that strong, she thought ruefully, climbing out of bed to wake Paola.

* * *

Iris was tidying up after breakfast while Paola attempted to put a pair of tights on by herself, a feat she was sure she could master, despite plenty of evidence to the contrary.

Her phone buzzed with a text message and Iris checked it absentmindedly, glancing out of her kitchen window, wondering how long the rain would hold off.

The message read, "I wish to take Paola to the zoo on Wednesday. A car will pick you both up at 11 a.m. Sergio."

Iris sighed. If Sergio was taking time off work to spend with his daughter, she figured matters might not run as straightforwardly as she'd hoped.

Well, the first thing to do was answer. She re-read the message, smiling despite herself at his perfect spelling and grammar and complete lack of "text speak." Once she'd replied, Iris emailed her agency to let them know she'd be unavailable for any last-minute jobs on Wednesday. It was inconvenient not to be able to work that day, but being a virtual secretary was usually quite flexible, and she didn't have anything urgent booked in. Her job didn't pay that well, but it meant she could work from home and fit it in around Paola's needs.

The good news was that he said the car would be picking both her and Paola up, so at least he didn't want to take their daughter off on his own. Of course the bad news was that he very rapidly appeared to be taking control of her life, something she really didn't want him making a habit of. But what could she do? Refusing to go would not only cause animosity, but possibly provoke him to fulfil his threat of legal action.

* * *

When the black limo pulled up outside her flat at precisely 11 a.m. on Wednesday, Iris wasn't at all surprised. Sergio was always punctual. She had everything ready and didn't wait for the driver to get out and knock on her door. Determined to show she could manage by herself, she struggled down the steps. Paola was under one arm, and in the other, the folded-up buggy, doing its best to open again, and a huge bag containing everything Paola could possibly need for the day. She knew she'd probably over-packed, but she wanted every eventuality covered so Sergio could see what a competent and organised mother she was.

The uniformed driver rushed over as quickly as he could while maintaining his dignity. She signalled she was alright, but he still insisted on opening the car door for her.

Sergio sat in the limo, busily tapping away at his phone. He glanced up and smiled at Paola, who called out "I'm here!" and immediately began to wiggle in Iris's grasp, wanting to explore the inside of the car and get closer to her father.

"You won't be needing that," said Sergio, gesturing towards the pushchair.

Iris bristled. Who was he to tell her what she would or wouldn't need for a day out with her own child!

"There'll be a lot of walking, she'll need a buggy," she responded as calmly as she could manage.

"I have one," he replied, as if it would be perfectly normal for him to carry a pushchair in the boot of his limousine.

"There was no need—" began Iris.

"There was every need," he interrupted. "That thing is cumbersome, unsafe, and, frankly, an eyesore."

"Fine," she said. There was no point in starting an argument before she'd even got in the car. Handing Paola over to Sergio, she dragged her buggy back up the steps and into her flat. When she returned, Paola was safely strapped into a very plush car seat.

Travelling by limousine was something Iris didn't think she'd ever get used to. The car practically glided over the roads, weaving delicately in and out of the other traffic despite its large size. She spotted a fridge next to Sergio, which she was sure would be packed full of goodies. Alone, she'd have happily explored it, but was embarrassed to do so in front of him. Even when he offered Iris a drink as he delved inside to find some orange juice for Paola, Iris declined. She kicked herself afterwards: why did she always have to be so stubborn when it came to Sergio, she wondered.

The car dropped them right outside the zoo's entrance, and the driver opened the boot, bringing out the new buggy. Sergio caught Iris staring at it open-mouthed.

"It's the best one for her age," he said defensively, anticipating her disapproval.

It's the most expensive for her age, thought Iris as she took in the design and Bugaboo label. Paola looked supremely happy and comfortable once she was all strapped in, but then came the awkward moment when they had to decide who was actually going to push. Not only did Iris want to be the one in charge, she was also dying to have a go with a buggy which might actually go in the direction she wanted it to. She staked her claim by somewhat awkwardly hanging her bags on the pushchair's back. She felt Sergio's eyes trained on her the whole time.

Apparently accepting that Iris had control, Sergio led them to the ticket booth and, despite Iris's protestations, paid the entrance fee for the three of them.

As they meandered at toddler pace through the zoo, Iris was amused to see how completely absorbed Sergio was in the animals: he appeared to be enjoying himself almost as much as his daughter. Paola meanwhile was in her element: two grown-ups competing to see who could make her smile the most was her idea of heaven.

Iris had to grant that Paola and Sergio were sweet together. They stopped to look carefully at each other every now and again. They seemed very comfortable, just content to be with each other, whether Paola was in the pushchair, or they were strolling along holding hands.

They were so happy that Iris felt the stirrings of jealousy beginning to surface again. She knew she was being silly and childish, but she'd always been the most adored person in Paola's life, and she felt like Sergio was trying to usurp her position. She was used to it just being the two of them, and that was something she was going to find very hard to let go of. Provided of course, she reminded herself, that Sergio didn't lose interest in Paola as swiftly as she suspected, and hoped, he would.

Iris made herself get more involved, although she felt she was interrupting almost. She knew much of the problem was that she just couldn't relax around Sergio: she felt his dark eyes on her whenever she was doing anything for Paola, and couldn't help but think he was judging her and how she cared for their child. She felt flustered, and became clumsy.

The one instance Iris thought she saw his confidence falter was when they sat down to lunch. Sergio with his olive skin and beautifully tailored clothes looked incongruous sitting at a plastic table, trying to decide what to order with chips. His suppressed discomfort was too funny; it was all she could do not to laugh.

Returning with a vanilla milkshake for Paola which she'd requested, Sergio was rather taken aback when after only a tiny sip, it was loudly declared "yucky" and demands were made for a chocolate one. He got up to get it, but Iris stopped him. She leant past Paola and took a taste.

"It's lovely sweetheart, drink it, please," she said kindly but firmly.

Paola's lip began to tremble, and she looked from Sergio to Iris, trying to decide if either of them would give in to a tantrum. Sensing weakness, she locked eyes with her father.

Iris could see he was wavering so she took control again, drawing her daughter's attention back to her with a firm, "Paola, I asked you to drink your milkshake."

Sensing this battle was well and truly lost, Paola took a deep slurp, then happily began to eat her food.

Iris was careful not to make eye contact with Sergio. She was worried he might have taken her stepping in as an attempt to undermine him, but she certainly wasn't prepared to have all her hard work in teaching Paola to be polite and well-behaved thrown down the drain. Having a rich daddy in her life who could buy her anything she wanted was no excuse for bad manners.

She snuck a glance at Sergio, and was rewarded with the comical sight of him peering at his meal with barely concealed disgust and mistrust. He prodded it with his fork as if to check it wasn't about to jump up and attack him. Catching her amused expression, he muttered something about bringing his own food on their next visit.

Paola ended up lasting until almost three, and then fell fast asleep in her buggy. Sergio was still animatedly chatting to her about the sea lions in front of them, not realising his audience was taking a break. Iris tapped him on the shoulder and indicated Paola's sleeping form. He tucked her blanket neatly around her so she wouldn't be cold, checking with Iris first that it was alright to do so. He really is very gentle with her, thought Iris.

Unsure what to do now, Iris awkwardly watched Sergio fussing over their daughter.

"Shall we get a coffee while she sleeps?" he suggested.

She checked her watch, hoping he'd get the hint that Paola falling asleep might be a sign they should leave.

He got her meaning, "We can't leave until she's seen the monkeys. I promised," he said firmly, but not quite as assertively as usual. For the first time since they'd met in the park, Iris felt she had some power in the relationship. He knew she could leave with Paola, and he couldn't really stop her, he wouldn't want to make a scene with people around and their daughter being tired was the perfect excuse for them to end their visit. Yet when it came down to it, Iris knew she couldn't bring herself to spoil her little girl's day, or make Sergio break his promise to her.

"Okay," she found herself agreeing. "Let's get a coffee and Paola can sleep for half an hour. Then I'll wake her up so she can see the monkeys. And then, we'll be going home," she added, so he wouldn't think her a total pushover.

While Sergio marched off to find the cafe again, Iris found a patch of grass for them to sit on under a shady tree and parked Paola's new buggy. Being a weekday, the zoo was remarkably peaceful and quiet apart from the odd group of school children wandering around with clipboards.

They sat in heavy silence sipping their coffees. Iris burnt her mouth drinking hers too quickly — the faster she drank up, the sooner they could see the monkeys and she could get home again, away from Sergio.

Eventually he spoke, "We make very beautiful children, I think."

"One very beautiful child," she corrected him quickly.

"Why did you give her a Spanish name?"

"When I first saw her, the name just came to me, it seemed a perfect fit."

"She must have been a charming baby," he said.

It seems the moment to have "the conversation" has arrived, thought Iris. Although she'd known it was coming, she felt supremely unprepared.

"I thought I was doing the right thing," she began, then paused, expecting Sergio to interject. When he didn't, she continued, "She wasn't exactly planned and, to put it bluntly, you didn't seem like very good father material. I didn't do it to hurt you."

"You have done a wonderful job with her," he commented quietly. "She's lovely."

"Thank you," she replied uncertainly.

"You are a very good parent," he continued. "I hope to learn from you."

She blushed, disconcerted by his praise, she wasn't sure how to respond. Yet again his eyes seemed to be boring into her, and the situation was getting uncomfortably intense. Iris sought an escape, and was grateful when the moment was broken by Paola waking up, taking the focus off Iris and back onto the zoo animals.

* * *

By the time Sergio's driver dropped Iris and Paola home, Iris didn't think she'd ever been more grateful to see her flat. It had been an extremely long day. She was pleased her daughter had obviously had a wonderful outing, but personally was very relieved it was now over.

Worried Sergio would want them to come back to his house for Paola's tea, Iris had got in first, reminding the driver of her address as soon as they'd reached the car. Sergio didn't argue the point.

Helping Paola out of the car along with the cuddly monkey and huge helium balloon she'd been bought, Sergio also carried the new pushchair up the stairs to the door of flat, "Please, keep it," he said, placing it on the doormat. He kissed his daughter then gave Iris a nod goodbye and again stated he'd be in touch soon.

Annoyingly, even when Paola was fast asleep, hugging her enormous monkey, Sergio's parting comment meant Iris couldn't fully relax. It had served to confirm that he didn't seem to be losing interest in his daughter. She suspected she and Paola would be hearing from Sergio again very soon.

Yet part of her still couldn't quite believe he'd taken a whole day off work to take Paola out. The Sergio she knew would very rarely even take a lunch break. He'd even seemed to have enjoyed himself, which was almost as much of a shock in itself.

What had happened to change him so dramatically? Was it purely the discovery of Paola? Or was there something else too? She'd probably never know, she thought sadly. Sergio was unlikely to open up to her about anything personal. She was surprised to realise that she really would love to know the answers, and not just for her and Paola, but to complete Sergio for her. Because now he'd never seemed more mysterious.

* * *

The anticipated phone call came two days later. It had already been a long day, Paola had a bit of a cold and so had been grizzly. She'd also asked to see Sergio, which had, perhaps irrationally, upset Iris — here she was caring for her daughter and doing everything she could to make her feel better, and all Paola seemed to want was someone else! And someone who'd only come into her life very recently.

Iris finally managed to get Paola to sleep at eight, by which point she'd realised that her own throat was hurting and she was feeling feverish. But because Paola had had to stay home from playgroup that morning, Iris hadn't been able to get her secretarial work completed for the day. Wearily she switched on her computer and settled down with a cup of hot lemon and honey to soothe her throat. She'd got comfortable and was beginning to become absorbed when the telephone rang.

Irritated, Iris snatched the phone, worried the noise would wake up Paola. She managed to croak a "Hello."

"Iris?" said Sergio's unmistakable voice.

"Yes, hi Sergio."

"You sound strange."

"I've caught a cold from Paola."

"Is she okay? Does she need a doctor?" he asked anxiously.

"It's just a cold, I'm sure she'll be much better in the morning."

"If not call me on my mobile. My doctor will see her immediately."

Iris heard Paola call out for her, and sighed, immediately blaming Sergio for having woken her by phoning.

"I've got to go, Paola's awake again," she said grumpily, putting down the telephone so Sergio could neither argue nor begin suggesting an ambulance ought to be called to deal with his daughter's sniffles.

Iris settled Paola down. She managed a couple of hours work then gave in and collapsed into bed feeling dreadful.

* * *

Next morning, it was Iris's turn to be roused by the ringing telephone. Realising how awful she felt, she decided to just let it ring; she'd call whoever it was back later. However, when the ringing didn't stop, she conceded defeat and hauled her aching body out of bed. It took her ages to make it down the stairs and to the phone, but it continued to ring. She picked up the receiver and cleared her throat, but before she could speak the voice at the other end said:

"Why aren't you answering your phone?"

"Sergio?"

"Yes," he answered impatiently, "Why aren't you answering your phone? Is Paola alright?"

Iris's throat felt raw as she managed to croak, "I was in bed."

She checked the clock hanging on her kitchen wall, it was almost eight.

"I'm not well, and it's early," she added for clarification.

"Is Paola alright?" he repeated crossly.

How would I know? I'm talking to you, thought Iris.

"She's in her cot, I'm sure she's fine."

"Have you checked on her?"

"No, I was in bed."

There was silence. Iris suspected Sergio was struggling to keep his temper.

"Would you like me to check on her now?" she asked wearily.

"If it's not too much trouble," he replied, a hint of sarcasm to his voice.

"Give me a moment."

With the phone in her hand, Iris climbed back up the stairs at a snail's pace, holding onto the rails to steady herself. She opened the door to her daughter's room. Paola was playing happily in her cot, chatting away to her teddies. She was obviously feeling a lot better. She gave her mother a huge smile and stood, putting her arms up and said, "Out, please!"

"She's fine," said Iris, unable to elaborate further as she was overcome with a fit of coughing. When it had subsided, and she'd regained her composure she heard

Sergio say, "I'll be over within the hour." He'd gone before Iris could voice her objections, which probably served her right, she thought to herself wryly, as she'd done the same to him the previous evening.

She put the handset down and lifted her daughter out of her cot. Carrying Paola safely downstairs sapped just about the last of Iris's energy. She put Paola in her high chair and managed to get her some juice, toast, and banana, then collapsed into a seat herself with a much needed cup of tea.

She glanced around with her sore eyes. The place didn't look too bad, she was naturally a tidy person, and did her best to keep the place nice. There was some washing-up in the sink, but she was grateful she'd managed to tidy up after Paola the previous evening. If Sergio really was determined to come round, at least she wouldn't be too embarrassed by her housekeeping skills.

True to his word, Sergio was outside Iris's flat half an hour later. She opened the door, noticing how annoyingly healthy and groomed he looked. Muttering something about his coming over being completely unnecessary, she shuffled back to the sofa, where she'd made herself a nest out of cushions and a blanket.

He followed, surveying the scene around him with interest. Paola glanced up from her toys. A big smile appeared on her face and she marched straight over to her father. He lifted her up, obviously delighted by the warmth of his welcome.

"Ciao, bella!" he exclaimed, checking her over for signs of illness. "You don't seem so sick!"

"I'm better now," Paola said cheerfully.

"I said she was fine," Iris pointed out, wishing he'd leave so she didn't have to feel embarrassed about being in her pyjamas.

Turning his attention to Iris, he glanced over and said, "You don't look good," somewhat bluntly.

"I know," she croaked.

"Go to bed," he ordered. She opened her mouth to object, but he continued, "Paola and I will be quite happy. You need some rest."

Iris wanted to protest more, but she felt awful and the thought of returning to her warm bed was very inviting. The prospect of leaving Paola alone with Sergio didn't fill her with the horror she thought it would, although a list of things he would need to know in order to look after Paola for an hour or so began immediately forming itself in her mind. But brushing them aside as fussing, Iris climbed off the sofa. She told Paola she'd see her later and pulled herself back up the stairs and into the haven of her bedroom.

She'd just got herself comfortable and was beginning to drift off to sleep, when she heard a firm knock on the bedroom door. Instantly she was wide awake again and sitting bolt upright.

"Yes?" she croaked.

Sergio opened the door.

"Is Paola okay?" she asked.

"She's quite alright, Iris, she has survived the last ten minutes with me," he answered with gentle sarcasm, "I thought you might need some tea."

Iris noticed a tray in Sergio's hands. Under normal circumstances, the idea of Sergio seeing her even further dishevelled like this and bringing her tea would have filled her with horror, but she felt so bad she was beyond caring, and the tea was certainly welcome.

As he placed the tray on the bed, Iris saw he'd also collected together some paracetamol and tissues, and even made her a slice of toast.

"Thank you," she managed to whisper.

"Is there anything else you need?"

Iris shook her head, and he gently closed the bedroom door behind him.

* * *

Waking up, Iris realised she felt quite a bit better, although her throat was still very sore. She looked at the clock and was amazed to see it was almost four — she'd left Sergio in charge of Paola for the whole day! Why on earth hadn't he come up to get her? Paola must be starving by now, she'd have missed her nap, and Iris dreaded to think the state her nappy must be in.

Iris climbed out of bed and went downstairs as quickly as she could, pulling her dressing gown around her as she went. The first thing she noticed was that Paola's new buggy was no longer parked in the hallway. Her stomach sank and her heart began to race. She called out to her daughter as loudly as she could manage and rushed through the sitting room and into the kitchen. The silence confirmed what she already knew — Sergio and Paola were gone.

Chapter 3

Iris took a deep breath to calm herself, but panic had already taken hold. One question forced itself to the front of her mind: would Sergio resort to kidnapping? She couldn't be sure but she suspected he might, and if he had abducted Paola she knew she had to act quickly. Trying her best to think clearly, Iris grabbed her mobile to call Sergio. If he didn't answer, she'd be straight on to the police.

Trawling through her messages to find his last text, she missed it twice, scanning the list too quickly in her flustered state. Finally she found it, her heart thumped loudly in her chest and her hands had begun to shake as she retrieved the number. She struggled to control her trembling hands before pressing *call*. However, just as she was about to push the button, the front door to her flat banged open and a voice shouted out "Mummy!"

Iris heard Sergio gently shush Paola and whisper, "Let's be very quiet, Mama might be asleep," as he manoeuvred the buggy into the flat.

Her heart still pumping hard, anger rose to the fore from her maelstrom of emotion, and Iris marched into the hall, all guns blazing. Unfortunately the effect was destroyed somewhat by the coughing fit she had as she tried to speak.

"Where the hell have you been?" she managed to ask, once her coughing had subsided.

"Excuse me?" he replied, completely calmly, but staring at her like she'd gone totally mad.

"Where have you been? I came down and you weren't here," she said, a little more meekly, realising how crazy she sounded.

Paola was struggling to get out of her pushchair, so Sergio bent down to help her. "We went for some lunch and then to the park, and a toy store." He gestured to a large Hamleys' bag hung on the back of the buggy.

"I thought . . ." she started to say.

"You thought I'd run off with Paola, and you would never see her again," Sergio stated.

"Yes," she admitted sheepishly.

He didn't comment, just removed the carrier bag and began folding the buggy brusquely, clearly annoyed, while Paola toddled off to play in the sitting room.

Iris thought she ought to explain herself: "I panicked. I didn't know you'd be taking her out, and you said that . . ."

She tailed off, not wanting to anger him further or remind him of the threats he'd previously made.

"I said I'd take Paola from you," he said sharply. "And I would, if it became necessary. Either through the courts, or otherwise."

He took a deep intake of air, as if doing his very best to control his temper. As he locked eyes with her, his ire seemed to make his irises even darker than usual. His nostrils flared slightly as he struggled to master his emotions and return his facial expressions to normal.

"If you're alright with Paola, I'll go. I have a lot of work to catch up on," he said stiffly.

He followed Paola into the sitting room to say his goodbyes.

Iris called out after him, "I'll be fine." Like he'd care, she thought crossly to herself as he left without giving her a backwards glance, just his usual ominous, "I'll be in touch."

Still feeling quite rotten, and with Sergio's threat hanging over her, Iris struggled to be "fun-and-entertaining-mummy" for the next few hours until it was time for a very tired Paola to go to bed. She sank gratefully onto the sofa once Paola was safely tucked up, and was forced to admit she really wouldn't have managed very well without Sergio's help. It was rare moments like this when she sadly reflected on how much she'd love a partner to support her in bringing up her beautiful daughter. It was so hard doing everything by herself, especially when she wasn't well.

Making a cup of tea, she let its warming magic restore some of her energy, and decided to tidy up. She noticed the large plastic bag lying on the floor in the hallway.

She picked it up curiously, wondering what Sergio had been buying Paola now. Opening the bag, she found a princess outfit complete with tiara. It was extremely pink and sparkly — Iris could just imagine Paola choosing it for herself. She took the dress out, and noticed another, smaller bag underneath it. Peeping inside, she discovered cold and flu tablets, throat pastilles, and Olbas oil. Sergio had visited a chemist for her. They were all adult medicines, so it wasn't that he'd been thinking about Paola. Just her. Pleased, if perplexed and also feeling a little guilty, she took a couple of the pills.

Thinking back, now she was in a calmer frame of mind, she knew she'd been rude to Sergio. But then, in her defence, she'd had a bit of a shock coming down to discover them gone, especially after the threats he'd made previously, and had now reiterated. What was she supposed to think? Yet wouldn't she also do anything necessary if she thought Paola would be kept from her? Wasn't Sergio merely putting into words what any parent would do? The fact was that she would have really struggled without him today, and she hadn't even thanked him. She'd overreacted and been ungrateful.

Resolving to do the right thing, Iris picked up the telephone, found his number, and called him. His mobile rang several times without response, and Iris was just about to give up and put down the receiver, when Sergio answered.

"Hi, it's Iris."

"I know. Is there a problem?"

"No, no. I just wanted to call to say thank you for today. And, um, to apologise for the melodrama."

"Oh, right."

There was silence. He was determined not to make it easy on her.

"I'm a lot brighter for the extra rest."

Again he didn't respond so she continued, "Paola had a great time with you, and the princess dress is lovely."

"She chose it herself."

"I gathered," said Iris, smiling.

When he didn't comment, she said awkwardly, "Um, I found the other bag. The one with the medicines."

"Good, I hope they make you feel better."

"Thanks, it was thoughtful of you to pick them up."

"I need to get back to work, but I shall see Paola soon."

"Okay," she said, grateful to end the stilted call.

She was pleased she'd made the effort to be nice. If they could at least manage to be civil to each other, things would be so much easier for Paola in the long term. As well as for Paola's parents. Maybe if she knew Sergio better she'd have trusted him more, and not jump to conclusions like she had that afternoon. Or at least know whether or not her concerns were justified.

Thinking back over the day, Iris realised it had been ages since she'd been looked after when she was ill. It had been years since someone had brought her a cup of tea in bed, or gone to the chemist to pick up some medicines for her.

Not having family close by to call upon, Iris was quite used to fending for herself, and usually considered herself pretty good at it, and mostly content with her life. She hadn't been in a relationship since her fling with Sergio. There were several reasons for that: pregnancy, and then caring for a young child, lack of time and babysitters. But top of the list was how hurt she'd been by Sergio. And however badly he'd behaved, no man since had ever measured up to him.

* * *

A couple of days later, Iris was almost completely back to normal. When she received a text from Sergio asking her to call him when she was free, she resolved to try harder to get on with him. After all, he was Paola's father, and, so far, his demands had been completely reasonable. Plus Paola wasn't a baby anymore and she'd pick up on any atmosphere — Iris didn't want her to feel she had to choose between them when she was older, especially because judging by how Paola and Sergio had bonded so quickly, Iris couldn't guarantee she'd be the one chosen.

Calling him back once Paola was napping, Iris waited anxiously for Sergio to pick up so she could start her new charm offensive. He answered with a brisk, "Iris, thanks for getting back to me."

"No problem at all, Sergio. How are you today?"

There was a brief moment of silence, presumably while he digested what she just said.

"I'm fine," he finally replied, sounding confused, then, returning to business, "I need to speak to you, are you free this evening?"

"Um, yes," she said hesitantly.

"Good, I shall come at eight, after Paola is in bed. Is that alright with you?"

"Sure. I'll see you then."

She was just about to put the phone down when, surprising herself, she blurted out: “Would you like me to make us dinner?”

Cringing at her outburst, time seemed to stop as she waited for Sergio’s answer, very unsure whether she’d done the right thing in offering to cook for him. It was only a very short time ago that she hadn’t even wanted to let him in her front door at all, and here she was encouraging him to stay for longer. Eventually, after what felt like an age, Sergio cautiously responded, “Yes, thank you, that would be very pleasant.”

Ending the call, Iris immediately began making a mental list of what she needed to do before Sergio arrived. If she started straight away, she could get quite a bit done while Paola slept and then run out to the shops later. Hopefully, she thought wryly, she’d be too busy to examine why she was going to so much trouble and how excited she was.

* * *

After a busy afternoon of shopping, cooking, and cleaning, Iris put Paola to bed early, and finally had a chance to get ready. Appraising her reflection critically in her dressing-table mirror, she didn’t think she looked too bad at all, and certainly not very different from when she’d worked for Sergio, and he must have found her attractive then, she mused. Why did she keep thinking of this as a date when it clearly wasn’t, she wondered to herself, noticing the butterflies in her tummy. Two people spending an evening together didn’t need to be romantic, and it made sense for her and Sergio to be friends and get to know each other better. Anyway, cooking dinner for him would be a good way to show how sorry she was for her overreaction when he’d taken Paola out.

She tried on a few outfits: she didn’t want to appear to have made too much effort, but she did want to look nice, especially as the last time she’d seen Sergio she’d definitely not been at her best. She was just debating whether to change again, or stick with the indigo-blue jeans and pale-pink V-necked jumper she had on, when she heard the doorbell. Giving herself a last glance in the mirror, she grabbed a necklace, putting it on as she rushed downstairs. She didn't want to risk Sergio ringing the bell again and potentially waking up Paola.

He smiled at her as she opened the door. He handed her a bottle of white wine and an amazing bunch of deep-red roses, which looked as soft as velvet. Maybe my feelings about this evening weren't so wrong after all, she thought.

Thanking Sergio, she invited him in. As he moved past her in the narrow hallway and took his coat off, Iris noticed how good he smelt. He'd obviously changed his clothes after work, as he wasn't wearing a suit. The open-necked dark-grey shirt suited him, she thought, making her stomach jump around even more.

Leading him into the kitchen, she went to open the wine, and recognised it as one she'd drunk with Sergio that evening they'd spent in the Italian restaurant. The night she became pregnant.

Sergio noticed her looking at the label, "You said you liked this wine, I think."

"Yes, I'm amazed you remembered," she replied, blushing.

He gave a small shrug, as if to say of course he'd remember. He locked eyes with her, but she pulled away. Just what's going on here, she wondered to herself. Was he trying to seduce her? Or was she trying to seduce him?

"Shall we eat?" she said quickly, breaking the growing tension between them.

"That would be lovely."

She served up the beef casserole she'd had on a low heat in the oven for the last couple of hours. He asked how Paola was.

"She's fine. Did her best to convince me to let her sleep in her princess outfit."

"I'm glad she likes it."

"She loves it: it's barely been off her."

She cut some bread and then sat down to join Sergio at the table. She noticed he'd refilled her wine glass.

"This is delicious," he said, in between mouthfuls.

"Thank you."

She found she was really enjoying herself: everything seemed so relaxed and as she glanced across at Sergio and caught him looking back at her, she realised, with a touch of concern, that all the old feelings she'd had for him were coming flooding back. He was very good company when he chose to be. She surprised herself by pushing the thoughts of how much he had hurt her firmly out of her mind. The wine and the atmosphere meant she felt powerless to fight her urges. As she listened to the seductive tones of his sultry Spanish voice, an image of them together with Paola, as a family, formed in her mind and a fierce longing for it to become a reality threatened to overwhelm her.

"The wine's gorgeous," she managed to say, worried he'd think her rude for not making conversation.

He smiled at her, and they chatted about Paola's playgroup, with Iris doing her level best to keep her treacherous feelings under control.

After they'd finished eating, she made some coffee. When she brought it through to the sitting room, Sergio was putting on a CD, and soon the smooth sounds of Ella Fitzgerald surrounded them. It was dark outside, and the table lamps created a warm, gentle, and rather romantic light.

They settled down onto the two-seater sofa. The wine mixed with his intoxicating smell, now they were so close, combined to make her feel quite light-headed. When his leg touched hers, she felt a jolt of electricity pass through her. She looked up and smiled at him, noticing a mischievous twinkle in his eye. She hoped she could guess what he was thinking.

"So," she said, doing her best to remain composed. "What was it you wanted to talk to me about?"

"Ah," he replied, seeming uncomfortable and taking a sip of coffee before continuing. "I must go to Barcelona soon, for business. I imagine I'll need to be there for some time."

"Oh," she said, deflated. Realising how despondent she sounded, she quickly added, "Paola will miss you terribly."

"You misunderstand me. I do not want to be away from Paola. I want her to join me."

"By herself?" asked Iris incredulously.

"You are of course welcome to accompany her. We will stay in my house in the city."

Suddenly it felt like there was a completely different man sitting next to her. He was back in business mode, and any flicker of fun or the desire Iris had thought she'd spotted earlier had completely disappeared. Her reaction to his announcement had put him on edge, and he was preparing for a fight.

"Never," she said, shocked to her core. "Why should I rearrange my life to suit you?"

"Because if you don't, you will make an enemy of me and you really don't want to do that."

"I'm not scared of you," she said, but there was a quiver in her voice. She didn't feel nearly as strong and confident as she was trying to sound. How could the atmosphere have changed so dramatically in a matter of seconds?

"I'm not asking you to be scared of me, but I want to be with my daughter. I won't let anyone separate us ever again, not even you."

"There's no question about you being able to see Paola," she said desperately, "But you can't seriously expect us to travel to another country."

"I do expect it. Obviously I will pay all your expenses; it won't cost you a penny."

"The money isn't the issue."

"Then I really don't see what is," he said with his usual finality.

No, she thought to herself, you truly don't, do you?

* * *

Drawing the evening to conclusion as swiftly as she could manage, Iris fastened the door firmly behind Sergio, wishing its locks could keep him out of her life for good. Returning to the living room, she let herself sink down into her sofa with a sigh: she felt completely emotionally spent. What an evening! What had she been thinking? Why had she tried to delude herself and put aside what he was really like? Was she so desperate for love?

Confused and lonely, she replayed the events over in her mind and actually found herself wondering whether she was being unreasonable — Sergio had been sure that he was in the right. But no, she was allowing him to see his daughter anytime he wanted, it wasn't her problem he needed to go and work in another country, and he couldn't expect her to just follow him wherever he decided to go.

Yet what could she do? She knew there was little point in her going through a reasoned argument: Sergio quite clearly had the power, and he knew it. If he said jump, that's what she'd better do, because if he wasn't happy, she dreaded to think how he might react.

He was not exaggerating when he'd told Iris he was powerful — she wouldn't stand a chance against his team of first-class solicitors, who were very helpfully devoid of ethics and willing to do pretty much anything for their extortionate hourly rate. What would such a battle do to her daughter, and how would she afford her own solicitor to fight her corner? Just how far would Sergio go to get custody of Paola? If it came down to it she knew he would fight, and fight dirty, for Paola, and he'd win.

Resigning herself, and trying desperately to think on the positive side, she thought hopefully the trip wouldn't be for too long — and it wouldn't cost her anything, after all. As long as she had internet access she could do her secretarial work anywhere. Maybe she should see it as a nice break — a break she'd never be able to afford on her own, she thought sadly.

But would staying with Sergio, and effectively being at his beck and call, really be much of a holiday? And how comfortable would she feel living in his house, especially after making such a fool of herself this evening? She'd read his signals completely wrong: they hadn't been connecting; he'd only been charming in order to soften her up so she'd agree to everything he wanted. He didn't want her kicking up a fuss. She was so stupid, falling for his tricks yet again! She'd acted like some silly teenage girl with a crush, not an adult with a daughter to protect. She could only hope he hadn't noticed quite how attractive she'd found him during dinner.

She marched crossly over to the kitchen table and blew out the candles, then dumped the plates into the sink. The clatter made her pause and listen out in case the noise had disturbed Paola. The flat was silent.

She continued clearing up, but was calmer now. It would do her no good just being angry. What she needed to do was convince Sergio that his idea was a bad one. For a start, presumably he'd have loads of work to do, in which case the last thing he'd want was a toddler running around the house, making all sorts of noise and mess. And what about when he wanted to bring women home? How would he explain his child and another woman living with him?

Maybe he'd agree to them just going to Spain for the odd long weekend? That wouldn't be ideal for her of course, but would certainly be better than potentially spending weeks in his house. And maybe on a weekend, Sergio might actually be able to spend time with Paola, something he wouldn't be able to do during the week. Surely he'd prefer that?

Perhaps she could get him to see how much his plan would disrupt Paola's world? It would upset her to take her out of playgroup for goodness only knows how long, especially when all she'd be doing was hanging around waiting for Sergio's attention.

The more Iris thought about it, the more she hoped she might have a chance to bring Sergio round to her way of thinking, to get him to see his scheme wasn't good for him or Paola. But she knew she mustn't rush things. She'd take a leaf out of his book and strike when he least expected it. She'd use the element of surprise and beat Sergio at his own game for once.

* * *

When Sergio next phoned to arrange to see Paola, he made no mention of the trip, and neither did Iris, who was resolved to lull him into a false sense of security. However, when he arrived at her home the following day, he made it abundantly clear that he wasn't going to let the matter rest.

"I assume Paola doesn't have a passport, so I had Serena pick up the forms. We can take her to get the photographs done this afternoon."

"Right," she said, thrown, but unable to come up with a convincing argument on the spur of the moment to derail this plan.

She hated his confidence that the matter was settled, that she'd go along with whatever he wanted, but she knew that was what she had to do. At least for now.

"I will have my secretary organise travel insurance for you both once we know the flight date. Will you email her your passport number?"

"Um, I don't have a passport," she said softly.

"You don't have a passport?" he repeated incredulously. "How is this possible?"

"I've never needed one."

"You've never had a passport? You mean you've never been out of the UK?"

"Never."

Seeing the look on Iris's face, he appeared to think better of continuing this line of questions despite his obvious curiosity.

"We can pick a passport form up from the post office and do your photograph with Paola's," he concluded.

She was too embarrassed to argue, he probably thought she was pretty pathetic not having a passport, and really boring for never having been abroad. He must have travelled to all sorts of far-off and exotic places.

Thankfully the topic was firmly closed by Paola calling out, "Papa, look!" and holding up her teddy to show him. Sergio smiled delightedly at Iris. It was the first time Paola had called him Papa, and he was obviously completely thrilled. He whisked the little girl up into the air and swung her around happily, "That's right, I'm your Papa!" Paola giggled away madly, loving that she'd made her father behave like this and calling out "Papa, Papa, Papa!" as loudly as she could. Their happiness was infectious and Iris found herself smiling and laughing along with them as Sergio danced Paola around the room.

* * *

Annoyed about the amount of effort she'd put into looking nice for Sergio when he'd come round to dinner, Iris had dressed very casually today — in jeans, a plain long-sleeved black top, and trainers, with her hair pulled back in a ponytail. Now she'd have to have her photo taken when she wasn't looking her best, a photo that would be in her passport for the next ten years! But she wouldn't humiliate herself further in front of him by explaining she needed time to get spruced up!

They walked to the high street, with Paola holding Sergio's hand, and Iris pushing the buggy. Several people smiled at them, thinking they made a picture-perfect young family. What did they know? Iris thought bad-temperedly.

Finding the post office mercifully empty, they picked up the passport form, and then headed to the photo booth in the nearby supermarket. In a moment of inspiration, she asked Sergio to watch Paola while she popped to the toilet.

Once safely in the ladies, Iris emptied her handbag out onto the side, sifting through the receipts, packets of raisins, and other debris to find something, anything, that might smarten her up for her picture. With the help of a hairbrush, lip gloss, and mascara she felt more photo-ready.

She turned her face from Sergio when she re-emerged, anxious not to let him know what she'd been up to. Naturally, in the five minutes she'd been gone, Sergio had bought something for Paola, in this case a chocolate bar, which she'd already managed to smear all over her cheeks. Thank goodness for wet wipes.

It certainly needed the two of them to ensure they ended up with an acceptable photo of Paola (the requirements for passport photos were quite stringent). The little girl's wiggling and a seat that seemed to have a mind of its own meant it wasn't an easy task.

When it was Iris's turn to have her photo done, her hair was definitely messier than when she'd left the ladies, but she couldn't really disappear again to sort herself out. Wanting the whole painful experience over and done with as quickly as possible, Iris accepted the first picture that was taken — she looked slightly manic, but it could have been a lot worse.

Sergio insisted that she fill out both sets of passport forms as soon as they got back to the flat. He made her a cup of tea and left her completing them while he played with Paola in the living room. Iris suspected he thought the forms might mysteriously "disappear" if he left them with her to send off at her leisure.

She tried not to appear too put out when he checked through the forms when she'd finished. Disgruntled, and feeling she was being treated like a child, she managed to keep her temper in check somehow — getting angry with him didn't get her anywhere and she needed to let this go, and work on changing his mind about Spain once she was sure he'd let his guard down.

* * *

Things went quiet for a week or so regarding the trip. The new passports arrived much faster than she'd expected, but Sergio said nothing about Spain on his frequent visits to see Paola.

Iris was grateful that he didn't take Paola out by himself again, even if she didn't particularly want to be watching from the sidelines while Sergio and Paola had fun together. She felt like the odd one out, and she really didn't like it. Still, Sergio didn't seem to mind her being there, and she'd much rather be with them than worrying about whether or not he'd bring Paola back.

Nevertheless, Iris liked to see Sergio and Paola getting along so well. She had to admit that he adored his daughter, and was doing a very convincing job of playing the doting father, even if she still wasn't entirely convinced it would last. She thought he overindulged Paola, but it was understandable given how new to being a dad he was. He was making up for lost time. She really couldn't complain about that.

One major benefit of having him around was having someone who enjoyed talking about Paola as much as she did. This was the first time she'd had anyone she could talk to her heart's content with about Paola.

However, she was even more wary of Sergio since the night of their dinner. She'd let her guard down far too much that evening, and was determined not to make the same mistake again. When he switched on the charm, it was all too easy to fall for it, and she knew how important it was that she kept her wits about her. She wouldn't let him blindside her again.

* * *

Cooking tea for Paola and herself early one evening, Iris heard her mobile ring.

"Hello," she answered.

"Hello. This is Bridget, I'm Mr Batista-Sanchez's secretary. A courier will be with you within the hour. I'm just calling to check you'll be home to receive the delivery."

"Yes, I'll be here," said Iris. "What's being delivered?"

"Tickets for yourself and your daughter. If you could check them over as soon as they arrive, and call me if there are any problems. I'll be in the office until about seven."

Iris took Bridget's number and got off the phone. So, he's chosen the dates he wants, she thought. She realised she should have asked Bridget when the tickets were booked for, but she'd look silly if she called back to find out now. Anyway, the courier would be here soon enough, she'd just have to be patient.

As with everything Sergio had a hand in, the courier arrived punctually. Opening the envelope, Iris's stomach sank when she saw the date on the two first-class tickets to Barcelona El Prat airport: departure was the day after tomorrow. Then she registered that the tickets were one way.

Chapter 4

After Iris had put Paola to bed, she thought about why exactly she was so shocked. She should have known Sergio would do something like this, it was just like him. He really didn't seem to feel the need to think about anyone other than himself. Why should he care that she had to arrange everything for her and Paola without knowing how long they were going for? All *he* had to do was instruct his secretary and housekeeper to prepare anything he needed. Their lives, despite now being so entangled, couldn't be more different.

It was rather too late for her slowly-slowly plan it seemed, so she resolved to immediately try to talk some sense into him. It would be just as awkward for him as for them, he was an important businessman who wasn't used to having a young child around. She couldn't imagine Paola fitting at all comfortably into his busy schedule in Spain.

Determined to make Sergio realise he couldn't always have his own way, particularly with something as big as this, Iris steeled herself and called his mobile.

He answered straight away with a wary, "Yes," as if he knew she was on the warpath. He certainly didn't seem surprised that she was calling.

She tried to highlight the difficulties and explain her alternative proposal, but not unexpectedly her words fell on deaf ears. She knew that when Sergio decided he wanted something to happen, it usually did, and as quickly as possible.

Trying to keep her temper, she pointed out how little time she had to prepare and pack.

Sergio replied that he'd let her know weeks ago that the trip was happening. "I've organised your tickets and passports, you don't need to book anywhere to stay. If you don't even want to pack, I will pay for whatever clothes and things you need when we are in Barcelona," he added testily.

She began to feel her frustration rise. He was making out that she was being unreasonable, when she was quite sure she wasn't! And of course she wasn't going to let him buy clothes for her, that was a ridiculous idea!

In desperation, though not really believing that it would make much of a difference to him, she brought up how inconvenient the trip would be for her: "What about my commitments? What about my life?"

"Stop being so melodramatic! It's only Europe, and it's not forever," he replied.

Grasping at straws, she threw out, "Well, what about my job then?"

Hearing him hesitate, she quickly continued, "I can't work from Spain, you know!" She crossed her fingers behind her back as this wasn't strictly true.

"What do you do?" he asked, seeming surprised Iris had a job at all, let alone one she'd be worried about. They'd never discussed what she did for money. Perhaps he just assumed she had some sort of independent means.

"That's none of your business," she answered crossly and somewhat irrationally.

There was silence for a moment as he calculated his next move.

"If necessary you will have to leave your job. I will give you any money you need," he declared.

"What?" She couldn't believe he would push her that far.

"I have missed two years of my daughter's life. I am not prepared to miss anymore."

She opened her mouth to respond but he continued, "Iris, you don't want to be against me."

A few seconds of silence ensued, during which they both seemed to be taking a deep breath and doing their best to remain rational.

"A car will pick you both up at eight in the morning on Friday. I myself am leaving for Barcelona tomorrow. I shall see you there Friday evening," he continued.

She furiously tried to think how on earth she could change his mind. He took a moment, seeming to appreciate just how angry she was and, with a sigh, changed tactics. "I just want to spend more time with my daughter," he explained calmly.

"You can, when you come back," she answered, also struggling to stay composed.

"I don't know when that will be."

"Why are you always so impatient?"

"Because I have no reason not to be. Enough of this, I must get back to work, I have a client waiting. I shall see you in Barcelona."

Iris knew she had no hope of winning the argument. Sergio had the upper hand: money. His money could buy him the means to have pretty much anything he wanted, including his daughter in Spain with him, for however long he wanted. Before she could think of a suitable retort, she realised he'd put down the phone.

* * *

When the telephone again rang early the next morning, Iris had a sneaking suspicion that it was Sergio calling. She was right.

"I've spoken to your boss," he stated, with no introduction.

"What?" she said, sleepy and not sure she could quite trust what she was hearing.

"The woman who runs the agency you work for. She said you can do your secretarial stuff anywhere," he said maintaining an exaggerated coolness.

"How did you even find out who I work for?"

"That's hardly the point. Can you work anywhere as long as you have a computer connected to the internet?"

"Yes, but . . ."

"But nothing, I don't have time for your silly excuses, I have a meeting to get to."

With that she found that he'd put the phone down on her, again.

She slumped down on the floor of her sitting room, and put her head in her hands. She was thoroughly fed up with having her life ruled by Sergio. How she missed the freedom she had before he'd come back into her life! Having a baby had tied her down, but at least she'd been in charge of her own life, and she adored Paola so much she could never begrudge any of the changes she'd made for her daughter. Now she was being pushed around, and she really didn't like it. Why, oh why did Sergio have to be in the park that day?

* * *

Iris's anger had by no means abated as the day of the flight arrived. She was absolutely furious as she packed for Barcelona. How had she managed to get herself into this ridiculous situation? She was a grown woman, a mother, and yet she was allowing herself to be bossed around by someone who was little more than a big bully. And she'd always been taught that you needed to stand up to bullies.

However, she was frankly too scared to contemplate the consequences of really standing up to Sergio.

Packing had been a nightmare. Not being sure how long they were going for, she had packed as much as she possibly could without having to pay extra baggage costs — she couldn't afford them, and her dignity certainly wouldn't let her recoup the money from Sergio.

Her area wasn't the safest in London, so she also worried about her flat being left empty. Plus, she was still cross with Sergio for doing his own investigations about her job, and embarrassed that her fib had been found out: she really could work anywhere as long as she had a computer Yet with the mood she was in, even this thought annoyed her — why was her life so easy to just pick up and move somewhere else? Was there no real substance to it? No roots to ground it. She had tried so hard to provide Paola with a proper, stable family home, but maybe she had failed.

However, despite everything, as Iris packed the last of Paola's clothes, she found she felt the tiniest bubble of excitement: yes, she was being forced to rearrange her life, but maybe her life needed rearranging. What did she actually have that was so important in London, apart from her wonderful daughter? A cramped and slightly damp flat in a not-so-good neighbourhood. Most of her friends had fallen by the wayside when she'd got pregnant, and the only family she had was her mother, who wasn't close by, and showed no interest in her daughter or granddaughter. She was getting an all-expenses-paid trip to a country she'd always wanted to visit. And surely it was a good thing that Paola's father wanted to be a part of her life. Just because things hadn't worked out between her and Sergio didn't mean that Paola shouldn't have a relationship with her daddy. She'd genuinely thought that not telling him about her was for the best. She'd never imagined Sergio would want to be a father, and thought he'd be nothing but damaging. He was proving her very wrong in that regard.

And yet, the nagging worry at the back of her mind wouldn't go away: Sergio had been so callous when it came to her feelings, what's to say he wouldn't treat Paola just as badly?

* * *

Later that day, Iris walked through the arrivals gate at Barcelona Airport, carrying a sleeping Paola in one arm, and pushing a trolley full of their luggage with the other. She glanced around anxiously, not quite sure who she was looking for, Sergio hadn't told her who they'd be met by. To her relief she heard a call of "Senora Brown!" She turned and spotted a smartly dressed, elderly man holding a card with her name on.

"Senora Brown?" he asked.

"Yes," she replied, managing to muster a small smile.

"Senor Batista-Sanchez sends his welcome, and regrets he was unable to be here to meet you himself. I am Miguel, his driver. Would you care to follow me to the car? Please let me deal with your baggage."

While she was only too grateful to allow someone else to push the heavy trolley, she felt awkward that it was someone she didn't know, and who seemed quite frail. Still, there wasn't an opportunity to argue the point, Miguel took charge of her trolley almost before he'd finished speaking.

He soon had Iris and Paola comfortably ensconced in the back of a beautiful Porsche Cayenne. A little boy's dream, all chrome and gadgets, the drive was so smooth it felt like they were barely moving.

"Your daughter is very beautiful," commented Miguel at one point, when the car was stopped at traffic lights.

"Thank you," Iris replied.

"She looks a lot like her father," he continued.

"Yes," she admitted, but stopped at that, not wanting to discuss her relationship with Sergio with a stranger. She was surprised that Sergio seemed to have told people about Paola, and pleased for her daughter that she was being acknowledged. She hadn't been sure whether he'd told his friends and colleagues.

"Here we are," said Miguel some time later, as they pulled up in a large, tree-lined square in the corner of which was a tall, rather imposing townhouse.

Miguel opened the door for Iris as she helped Paola out of her car seat. The street itself was quiet, but there was plenty of background noise from the city around. Strangely these sounds were quite different from the London hubbub she was used to, more exotic somehow.

Iris was shocked by the heat, despite it being after three in the afternoon, as she stepped out of the air-conditioned cocoon. Miguel signalled to Iris to follow him into the townhouse. Paola didn't seem bothered by the temperature, but gazed curiously around her as Iris carried her up the steps to the front door. They entered a large communal hallway, at the far end of which was an elevator. Using a key to access the top floors of the building, Miguel operated the lift. They were greeted at the top by a friendly, cheerful woman, who introduced herself, in reasonable English, as Consuela, Sergio's cook and housekeeper. As well as being far older than her counterpart back in Sergio's London home, Consuela was also a great deal plumper. Iris automatically warmed to her.

The inside of the house was like a cool sanctuary from the heat and noise of the city below. Iris felt relief to be out of the warmth of the street as she took in the amazing tiled floor underfoot and the ornate mouldings on the ceiling. The décor fitted the property perfectly, everything was big and bright from the huge vases of fragrant lilies gracing each walnut tabletop, to the massive, baroque gilt mirror on one wall, which Paola was thrilled to catch sight of her reflection in. The apartment seemed endless; Iris lost count of the number of rooms running off the hallway she was led through.

Consuela fussed over both Iris and Paola, good-naturedly ushering them into the kitchen, where she made a delicious coffee for Iris, gave Paola some juice, and then produced a tin of home-made madeleines.

Iris caught Consuela peering closely at the little girl as she munched on her snack. "She's so like her father," Consuela muttered to herself with a smile.

Paola appeared to be enjoying Consuela's attention and the cakes in equal measure.

As Consuela and Paola played peekaboo, Iris took a further chance to look around. The kitchen was modern, despite the clear age of the building, and bright, with a large table in the centre — Iris liked it much more than the kitchen of Sergio's London home, which seemed rather cold and sterile by comparison. A couple of pots bubbled away on the stove, and a soft hint of Consuela's baking hung in the air.

Once Consuela decided they were suitably refreshed, she led them up a beautiful, sweeping staircase to their rooms on the next floor of the apartment.

Iris had been expecting to be sharing with Paola, but they had a large bedroom each. They had their own huge bathroom, complete with a roll-top bath in the middle so big that Iris was sure Paola would think it was a swimming pool.

Their luggage had been brought up and put on their beds by Miguel, Iris assumed, which made her feel guilty again. Miguel didn't look strong enough to carry so much as a bag of shopping, it didn't seem possible that he'd managed to lug the heavy suitcases up the stairs.

Consuela left them to unpack. Iris emptied out Paola's rucksack containing her favourite toys, which the little girl pounced on as if she hadn't seen them for years. Next, she unpacked Paola's suitcase and began putting her clothes away in the chest of drawers, while her daughter played happily and chatted away to herself on the floor. Iris thought if she got Paola's stuff sorted out first, she'd be able to pop her into bed as soon as their long journey caught up with her.

Bending down to put a dress in the bottom drawer, Iris was caught unawares when she heard a squeak of excitement from Paola. She spun round to see Sergio in the doorway. She self-consciously pulled her top down where it had ridden up at the back.

The little girl was obviously thrilled to be reunited with her father. She jumped up, giggling, into his ready arms and happily accepted the hug and kiss he offered. As she watched the pair, Iris was struck once again by the similarities between them.

"Oh, how I have missed you, my darling," Sergio said, letting Paola clamber down. She pulled him out into the hall. She led him downstairs to the kitchen, babbling away happily about her need for a banana and a lot else which not even Iris could decipher as she followed.

As Paola happily munched on a banana, Sergio turned to Iris and asked: "I trust you had a good journey?"

"Yes, thank you."

"Did you enjoy your first flight?" he continued into the silence.

"Yes," she answered. She looked at Sergio's face carefully, checking for signs of mockery, but surprisingly found none. "Paola slept for most of the flight. I think it helped being in first class, although you really needn't have spent so much on the tickets," she added quickly.

"Only the best will do for my girl," he said, gazing indulgently down at his daughter.

"Your home is gorgeous," said Iris, more for something to say than wanting to make a compliment.

"Thank you. I am very fond of it, and of Barcelona as a whole. This area is known as the Gothic Quarter, it contains some astounding architecture."

"Gothic Quarter sounds a bit spooky," she replied.

He frowned. "You don't like this city?"

"I don't know it," she countered, and was surprised to see a flash of hurt in his eyes.

"Well, I'm sure you'll grow to love it soon," he said with his usual certainty. He carried Paola back upstairs so she could play with her toys while Iris finished unpacking.

"I see you're settling in," he said, indicating the empty suitcase on the bed.

"Yes, thanks," Iris replied, determined to be polite to Sergio in front of their daughter, even if she was still silently seething at being forced to drop everything to come here.

Sergio sat down on the floor with Paola to be shown her toys, all of which he'd seen before.

"Is there anything you need?" he asked, as he helped Paola make a tower with her blocks.

Iris wondered whether he was being so nice because he felt a bit guilty about her being there, but swiftly dismissed the thought. He'd made his feelings perfectly clear about the trip and what he expected of her. She really doubted he'd suddenly start to see things from her point of view, not when he'd been so sure he was in the right.

"I think we've got everything, thanks. Consuela seems really nice."

"Shall I ask her to begin preparing tea for Paola?"

"I can do it if she's busy," she said, not wanting to make extra work for Consuela.

"Whatever you like," he said with a shrug. He was clearly determined not to fight today.

The argumentative part of her was tempted to entertain itself by seeing how far she could push him, but her sensible, grown-up side warned her not to rock the boat.

Iris found Consuela busy in the kitchen, pre-empting her request for Paola's tea.

"The children here in Spain, they eat very late, but I think your little one will be hungry and tired now?"

"Yes, thank you," replied Iris with a smile.

"Signor told me Paola's favourite foods so I could get them."

"How very thoughtful," Iris said, her smile forced now — why did Sergio always have to be so controlling?

"I would like to make her tortilla. I think she will like it."

"That sounds lovely."

"And you will eat later with Signor?" enquired Consuela. "He requests I make paella for your first night."

"Oh, thank you, that sounds wonderful," she said, although she really didn't relish the thought of a later supper with Sergio after the long day she'd had. She'd much rather just eat with her daughter and then have a long bath and settle into bed for an early night. She was too tired to be polite and on her best behaviour during their dinner, or to be sure of keeping her defences up in case Sergio planned to catch her with her guard down again.

* * *

Paola enjoyed the tortilla, but she was almost asleep in her chair by the time she'd finished her dessert, and was more than ready to begin preparing for bed.

Sergio had disappeared, presumably to wherever his study was so he could get some more work done. Iris wasn't sure whether he'd want to be called so he could do Paola's bath and stories, or at least come and give his daughter a kiss goodnight.

It was also hard to know what Consuela was used to doing for guests, and whether she'd be offended if Iris took over. She seemed so nice that Iris really didn't want to upset her, but having never had a housekeeper herself, she was unsure of the etiquette.

Consuela had disappeared as Paola was eating; she'd gone to run a warm, very bubbly bath for her, even heating up towels on the towel rail so they'd be toasty when the little girl got out of the water. She explained to Paola they didn't have any bath toys here yet, but she'd found some plastic tubs and bottles for the child to play with.

Just as Paola had almost finished her bath, and Iris was debating whether or not to ask Consuela where Sergio was, or if she could watch her daughter for five minutes while she went to find him, he appeared at the doorway.

"Hello there, my little mermaid," he said smiling at Paola.

Turning to Iris he explained, "I needed to make a couple of business calls, but I am all finished now, shall I do her stories?"

"Sure," said Iris, "I'll just go and get her pyjamas ready if you want to get her out and dry her."

A couple of minutes later, Sergio came into Paola's bedroom, carrying a very giggly little girl wrapped in a huge fluffy towel.

"I don't have any books here for her yet," said Sergio with a worried expression on his face. "I was hoping we could go out shopping for some toys and stories tomorrow, if that's ok."

"I've brought her favourites with us, they should be enough for while we're here," said Iris, pedantically.

"Iris, you should know by now that it gives me great pleasure to buy things for our daughter," he said gently. "I'd like her to choose some things for while she's here. I promise I won't go mad," he added with a wink that sent shivers through her. No matter how determined she was not to react to him, her body had other ideas.

With a sigh, she conceded, "Shopping tomorrow would be fine."

"Great, we'll set off late morning and go for lunch at a pizza restaurant Paola will love."

Not really sure what to do with herself while Sergio was reading to Paola, Iris went into her room and began on her own unpacking.

She couldn't help but smile at how different the books she'd read out loud hundreds of times sounded in Sergio's strong Spanish accent. When he'd finished, she heard him tell Paola they were going shopping tomorrow and he'd find her some Spanish stories.

A minute later, and much to Iris's amusement, Sergio called out "Mama! Paola's ready for her goodnight kiss."

"Ok, Papa!" Iris answered as she came into the bedroom, not able to hide the mischievous grin on her face.

He looked embarrassed, so Iris gave him a smile to reassure him he hadn't done anything wrong, although she didn't think she'd ever get used to the stern businessman she knew referring to her as "Mama" — something he did so frequently in front of Paola that the little girl was now using it instead of "Mummy." She sounded so sweet when she said it; Iris couldn't bring herself to be cross about her new title.

After her daughter was happily tucked up, Iris again wasn't sure what was expected of her. Should she go downstairs and offer to give Consuela a hand? Should she dress up for dinner? When would dinner be? She knew that people in Spain ate later than in England, but how late was late?

Luckily the problem was solved by Sergio asking if she'd like to join him for a glass of wine.

If possible, the kitchen smelt even better than before. Consuela was busy at the stove. She'd set out some bread, tomatoes, and olives on the table. Sergio offered her a glass of wine. She accepted it but continued cooking, not joining them at the table.

The olives were delicious, and Sergio showed Iris the traditional Catalan way to eat the bread and ripe tomatoes, rubbing the cut tomatoes roughly across the bread, until it was saturated with the sweet juice and seeds.

The wine relaxed her, and she was forced to admit she was actually enjoying herself. In fact, she was having a far nicer evening than if she'd been sat by herself at home with her usual microwave ready-meal. She appreciated that

Sergio and Consuela were talking as much as possible in English, the pair only resorted to Catalan if there was something Consuela either didn't understand or wasn't sure of the English for.

"How long until supper is ready?" Sergio asked Consuela.

"Ten minutes."

"Perfect. Come," he said to Iris. "There's something I wish to show you."

She followed Sergio upstairs to the first floor; they both tiptoed as they went past Paola's room. They crept along to the end of the corridor, where two doors faced them. Sergio opened one and gestured for her to go through. The room she found herself inside was quite different from the rest of the house. Sloping ceilings and two small attic windows, coupled with packed bookcases around all the walls, gave the space a cosy feel. In front of one of the windows was a heavy, antique mahogany desk and what looked like a supremely comfortable wing-back leather chair. A laptop and a brass lamp sat on the desk. A pale-pink chaise longue completed the room.

"This is for you to work in while you are here. Is it suitable?"

Looking around in delight, Iris gushed, "Yes, it's wonderful," before she had a chance to control her emotions. "Are you sure it's alright for me to work?"

"It's fine. Consuela can babysit Paola whenever you need to work. Or if you prefer there's a private crèche nearby."

"You've thought of everything."

"You said you needed to work, so I am making that possible for you."

"Thank you," she said, "I appreciate it."

"Let me know if there's anything else you need up here and I'll arrange it."

Catching his eye, she smiled at him, pleased to feel he was treating her as an individual, someone more than just Paola's mother.

* * *

When she woke up the next day, Iris felt disorientated, not least because sunshine streamed through the gaps in the window shutters in stark contrast to the usual grey London mornings. Checking her watch, she was surprised to see how late it was. She hadn't slept in properly since Paola was born: being the single mother of an early riser was definitely not conducive to lie-ins. Her daughter must have been exhausted by all of yesterday's excitement not to be up yet.

She got up and wandered into Paola's room. She was surprised to see the bed empty: where was Paola? Was she hiding? Iris called out to her but there was no reply. She quickly searched the room, but found no trace of the little girl.

Oh no, what if Paola had woken up early and Iris hadn't heard her open her bedroom door? This was why she hadn't moved Paola into a bed at home but was keeping her in her cot for as long as possible.

Her first concern was that Paola might have woken Sergio up at some ridiculously early hour, which she was sure he wouldn't appreciate. Then again, a more pressing worry was that Paola could have gone downstairs by herself; there were no stair gates to stop her here. Reassuring herself that Paola hadn't hurt herself on the stairs as she would have heard her daughter's cries, Iris hurried out into the hallway. Sergio's room was closest so she decided to check there first.

Iris knocked on his bedroom door. The thought did occur to her very briefly that she must look a state having only just got out of bed, but that really wasn't important now. When he didn't open the door, or call out, on the second knock, Iris took a deep breath and went in.

The bed was neatly made and Sergio was most definitely not in it. Giving the room a quick scan and seeing Paola was not there, she headed downstairs, the kitchen was the next most likely place to find her.

"Paola, Paola!" she called out.

"Iris?" Sergio's voice came from below.

Peering over the banisters into the hallway, she saw Sergio and Paola gazing up at her with identical bemused expressions on their faces.

"We've been making pancakes," Sergio said. "We were just coming to ask if you wanted any when we heard thumping and running."

He paused, and looked pointedly at Iris, clearly expecting an explanation for her bizarre behaviour.

"I couldn't find Paola," she eventually muttered, feeling very embarrassed to be seen in her pyjamas and to have been in bed while Sergio looked after her daughter. She skulked back to her room to tidy herself up, before joining the happy pair for breakfast.

* * *

Later that morning, the trio set out to buy Paola a few "necessities." Miguel was waiting outside the house, with the car parked in the square. The day was already pretty warm, and Iris was once again glad of the vehicle's air conditioning as they headed to the Diagonal Mar shopping centre.

By now Iris knew there was absolutely no point in trying to restrain Sergio when it came to him spending money on his daughter. She soon lost track of how much he'd spent, but tried to take pleasure in the fun Paola was having, rather than fixating on how she'd never be able to afford these things herself.

Sergio seemed to particularly enjoy picking out storybooks for Paola, especially when he found favourites from his own childhood lurking on the shelves of the bookshop. Most of the purchases were left in the stores to be picked up later, presumably by Miguel, but Paola insisted on taking her new doll and its stroller with her. She toddled along, pushing the stroller, with a parent on either side.

They left the shopping centre and were driven back into the centre of the city. Miguel dropped them off on a side street just off La Rambla, and Sergio led Iris and Paola to a family-run pizzeria. The restaurant was small and seemed very dark after stepping in from the bright sunlight. It took a moment for Iris's eyes to adjust. It consisted of only about seven tables, plus the two they'd passed outside. They were shown to the one free table after Sergio had been warmly greeted by practically everyone who worked there. He was clearly an old friend.

It was soon obvious that Sergio had made a very good choice for lunch. The restaurant was relaxed enough for Iris not to worry about Paola being a nuisance — on the contrary, the waitresses made a huge fuss of the little girl — and the food was excellent. With three courses and coffee, they were there for almost two hours, and Iris was pleasantly surprised at how well Paola behaved and amused herself with her new doll. Sergio was friendly, and Iris found herself really enjoying the meal and his company. He was so easy to be around when he was like this — carefree and fun. And with another adult around to help entertain Paola, she actually got to eat her food while it was still warm.

* * *

Despite the next day being Sunday, Iris thought she ought to try to get a few hours of work in. She was behind because of the trip to Spain.

After breakfast, Paola happily played at the kitchen table with some dough Consuela had made. Reassured by the housekeeper that she'd be delighted to watch Paola for a while, Iris went upstairs to her new study. She was just beginning to get properly immersed in the work, and was enjoying the luxury of having a whole office to herself, when there was a knock at the door, and Sergio came in.

"I thought I'd take Paola out for a while to the Parc de la Ciutadella. My friend recommended it, his daughters like it very much," he said.

"Oh, right," she replied, a hint of uncertainty in her voice.

Sensing she wasn't entirely comfortable with his plan, he added, "Would you like to come?"

She did want to go: Sergio taking Paola out by himself in London was bad enough, but for him to do so here, in a country many miles from home and where everyone spoke a language Iris didn't understand, was pushing her trust in him to its limit. In the worst case scenario, she'd really have no chance of finding Paola if Sergio decided to hide her daughter from her in Spain. But if this dysfunctional family set-up was going to work, she needed to have faith in him, and keep a lid on some of her own insecurities. And aside from that, if she didn't really knuckle down to her work today, she knew she'd end up in a bit of a mess. She took a deep breath and said quickly, before she could think better of it, "No, thanks, I'd better crack on. You two have fun."

"We will," he said, seeming surprised, even pleased, by Iris's response. "See you later." He left swiftly, probably to make sure Iris didn't have a chance to change her mind.

* * *

There really had been no point to Iris staying behind: she couldn't focus and constantly thought about what Sergio and Paola were getting up to. Had he remembered everything their daughter would need? Had he put on her sun cream? What if he was distracted and she ran off? She might be run over. The streets of Barcelona were so busy, and a lot of the drivers seemed to be complete maniacs, as far as she could tell.

Of course once she started fretting, it was very hard to stop her thoughts spiralling out of control. She even went so far as to check she still had Paola's passport, panicking again that Sergio might try to kidnap her. She appreciated that this was rather far-fetched: who'd kidnap a child from a mother who was staying in the kidnapper's house?

She clock-watched the entire afternoon, barely touching the lunch Consuela brought up for her. Iris tried to work out when she should expect Sergio and Paola back, as that time passed she really began to worry.

Finally, when her emotional state was approaching the point where she was wondering what the number for the emergency services was, she heard the lift arrive, and the sound of happy voices drifted up from the hallway.

Iris felt her whole body relax. She'd overreacted ridiculously once again. She knew she had to stop behaving like this. For her own sanity as much as anything else, she had to force herself to trust Sergio, and believe that, if nothing else, he wanted what was best for Paola. He'd told Iris that he thought she was a good mother, if he really meant that, surely he wouldn't try to take Paola away from her, not without provocation anyway.

She waited a few minutes before going downstairs so Sergio wouldn't think she was hurrying down to check on them, and saw Sergio and Paola cuddled up on a sofa together looking at one of Paola's new Spanish books. Unnoticed, she watched the contented pair. She couldn't help wondering whether she'd been wrong to keep them apart. They obviously loved each other very much, and Sergio was right that he'd missed out not knowing Paola as a baby. He'd never have those precious experiences. Although at the time she'd felt differently, she worried now that her motives had been selfish: hurt by his actions, she hadn't wanted to risk further pain. Possibly, she'd known she could handle him rejecting her, but not their child. However, witnessing the bond forming between the father and daughter made her rethink everything she'd been so certain of when she'd seen the pregnancy test result three years ago.

* * *

Iris's softening towards Sergio was soon put to the test. The apartment was beautiful, and she was enjoying getting to know Barcelona, but couldn't shake the feeling that she wasn't truly "free." Sergio never stopped her doing anything or going anywhere, it was more that the only reason she was in Spain in the first place was because of him: she felt tied to him and anchored by his wishes. A week after she and Paola had arrived, the matter came to a head when Iris commented during supper that she and Paola had been to the children's museum.

"You seem to be enjoying the city," he replied.

She was tired and his comment hit a sore spot.

"Well, I may as well at least try to make the most of having to be here," she retorted grumpily.

He looked taken aback, but calmly took another mouthful of food, chewed it thoughtfully, and swallowed, before responding carefully, "You make it sound like you are a prisoner."

"Well, maybe it seems like that sometimes."

"I'm sorry you feel that way. That certainly was not my intention."

"You've made us very welcome, and been more than generous," she conceded, hardly able to continue being angry with him while he was so composed and considered. "But I do feel forced to stay here."

"Is my home so terrible? Here Paola has everything she needs," he said incredulously, losing some of his cool demeanour.

"Paola never wanted for anything, living with me, you make it sound like she was neglected!" she said, immediately picking up on the negative strain of his remarks.

"You live in a tiny flat in a bad area," he replied matter-of-factly.

"The flat's fine, and so is the area. You're being rude." As she said this, she became aware that the conversation had definitely got out of hand. She knew she wasn't helping herself, and her words were making the situation worse, but she just couldn't seem to stop.

"It may be fine now, but Paola will not want a bedroom the size of a wardrobe when she's fourteen."

"Well, when she outgrows it, we'll move!"

"How? With what money? How are you going to send her to a good school? Pay for university? Take her on holidays?"

"We'll manage," she said testily, reluctant to admit there was some truth in what he was saying. Why did he always have to be so infuriating?

"But why 'manage' when she can have so much more?" he asked.

"Because money isn't everything."

"You think that now."

"No, I know that. Paola is very loved, and I'll do whatever it takes to make sure she has everything she needs as she grows up. I'll work two jobs if I have to."

"And never see Paola because you're always working?"

"We'll manage."

"There's no need for you to just 'manage'! I am here to help."

"You're Paola's father, it's great you want to play a big part in her life, but I don't need your money!" She got up and said stiffly, "I've had enough supper, thank you," before sweeping out of the kitchen.

She stalked up to her room in high dudgeon, and was alone but for her rumbling stomach. She thought with consternation of Consuela's delicious food and her unsated hunger. Oh blast, and the book she was reading was downstairs on one of the hall tables — well there was no way she was going back down! She guessed she was in for an early night.

She tiptoed into Paola's room to check on her. Paola looked so sweet tucked up in her blankets, but also so like Sergio. She hoped her little girl would grow up with the right sort of values, and not be as motivated by money as her father. Now that Sergio was on the scene, it seemed Paola would never want for anything materially, she'd have plenty of things, but Iris wasn't sure this wouldn't cause other problems along the line.

* * *

Iris heard Sergio leave for work early the next morning. She was glad: she'd calmed down, but didn't fancy breakfasting with him. The longer she could go before seeing him, the better.

As she watched Paola eat her breakfast and chatted to Consuela, she felt her spirits lift, and she planned what they'd do that day. She needed to get some work done, but there was plenty of time for an outing first.

However, her good mood wasn't destined to continue. The phone rang as they were about to set off to a park Consuela had told Iris about. Consuela answered it, but called out to Iris that it was for her, just as they were going out of the door. Puzzled as to who, other than Sergio, would be calling her on the landline, Iris took the call, with a questioning, "Hola?"

"Hola, this is Senor Barista-Sanchez's secretary, Carmen. Senor Barista-Sanchez has asked me to check whether adjoining rooms in the George V will be fine for you and your daughter next week?"

"The George V?"

"Yes, the hotel. In Paris."

"I wasn't aware that I was going to Paris," said Iris.

"Shall I book the rooms?" enquired the secretary again, sounding confused.

"No!" said Iris, perhaps a bit too sharply, but determined that Sergio was not going to boss her around. "I don't know what Ser—, Senor Barista-Sanchez has planned for himself, but Paola and I will not be joining him."

Clearly surprised by Iris's reaction, Sergio's secretary politely said she'd let Sergio know, then ended the call.

Iris spent most of the day planning what she was going to say to Sergio when he got back from work. She half expected him to call from his office so they could argue it out over the phone. Just in case, she switched her mobile off while she and Paola were out — she certainly didn't relish the thought of standing in the middle of a busy park, trying to keep an eye on her daughter as she contended with Sergio on the telephone.

* * *

Sergio returned home as Paola was finishing her tea. By unspoken agreement, they didn't mention the Paris trip in front of the little girl. As usual, when he wanted something, Sergio seemed to be making an extra effort to be nice to her. She had some work she needed to email off that evening, so he offered to do Paola's bath and stories so she could get it done before supper.

Once Paola was ready for bed, Sergio called Iris to come and say goodnight, and asked if she'd join him for a drink. She was tempted to say no, using the excuse of her unfinished work. But she'd completed the bulk of it, and she couldn't avoid talking to him forever. Consuela had left for the day and, now that Paola was in bed, it was as good a time as any to talk to him.

As straight-talking as ever, he got right to the point as he poured them both some wine: "My secretary tells me you and Paola won't be coming to Paris with me."

"That's right," Iris replied, taking a sip of wine.

"Do you mind telling me why?" he asked calmly.

They seemed to be skirting around each other, sizing each other up, like boxers at the beginning of a bout.

"We've already followed you to Spain, I don't see why we should have to pack up again and follow you to France," she explained. "Especially when you can't even be bothered to ask me yourself, you just get your secretary to call and tell me what I'm supposed to be doing! You could at least have given me some notice."

"I only found out this morning, I didn't have a chance to phone myself, so I had my secretary do it so you'd know what was going on. I really don't see the problem."

"Well, thank you so much for informing me of your plans for my life," she said.

He looked confused.

"I would expect for you to ask whether Paola and I *want* to come with you to Paris," she clarified.

He gave a small, tight smile, "Okay, then. Iris, would you and Paola like to come to Paris with me next week?"

"No."

He sighed with frustration.

"We aren't able to come to Paris with you."

"And why not?" he demanded.

"We're too busy."

"You can work anywhere, and Paola is two, she has nothing to be busy with!"

"We've already come here, it's not fair to make us up sticks again!" she said angrily. She was finding it difficult to control her temper. She wanted to be calm and collected and put her arguments together eloquently, but she always seemed to fall to pieces when she argued with Sergio.

"Up sticks?" he queried.

"Yes, 'up sticks' — to go, to pack up, to move."

"Oh, Santa Maria! You're not moving, it's just a short trip for a few days!" he said.

She was pleased to see he was losing his cool faster than she was.

"It's more upheaval for Paola, she's not some sort of toy you can just cart around with you wherever you want."

"I want her with me."

"No, I have work to do and plans for next week. I'm not dropping everything just so I can follow you to Paris."

"Never have I known a woman like you. I offer to take you and your daughter to a beautiful city, to pay for you to stay in one of the world's finest hotels. Anyone would think I was threatening you with terrible privations!"

"I'm not coming."

"Fine. I shall go alone."

It was Sergio's turn to storm out of the kitchen. He left muttering darkly to himself in Catalan.

Goodness, that went well, Iris thought. She couldn't believe she'd actually won an argument.

* * *

True to his word, the following week, Sergio went to Paris by himself. He was only gone for three nights, and he called every day to speak to Paola, but the little girl missed him terribly.

Iris was proud of herself for standing up to him; until she thought about how empty the evenings felt without Sergio around, and how she'd turned down a trip to a city she'd always dreamt of going to and might not have the opportunity to visit in the future. She yet again pledged to try harder with Sergio and stop being so pig-headed, but feared that it might not be long until she broke the resolution once more. He just seemed to have a gift for getting under her skin.

Still, when he returned from Paris, she accepted, with genuine graciousness, the perfume he'd bought her, and thanked him for the presents he'd brought back for Paola. If he was surprised by her mood change, he didn't say so, and eventually she gave up waiting for him to mention it.

Chapter 5

Always having had Paola to herself, Iris wasn't surprised she'd resented the addition of another person in their life, usurping her role and dividing Paola's affections. And while this had certainly been true at first, she discovered that she relished having someone else to share the pressures of parenthood with, as well as its many joys. It was lovely to sit down at the end of the day and chat to Sergio about how wonderful the mini-person they'd created together was. Eventually, as they'd become more comfortable with each other, these talks veered onto topics other than Paola, and Iris found she looked forward to them, although they were tinged with regret.

Iris had only worked at Sergio's company for a couple of months before she'd left, but she'd been a quick learner, and she'd swiftly found out a lot about it. After a day at the office, she and Sergio would go for dinner and talk for hours about all sorts of things, often business. He'd seemed to confide in her completely. Unlike now. She missed that intimacy and felt he no longer trusted her enough to open up to her. He never mentioned work if he could help it, and changed the subject if she brought it up.

He seemed to be doing his absolute best to keep his business and home life completely separate.

He left early for his office each morning, though always after having breakfast with Paola first. He only seemed to switch into work mode as he picked up his briefcase on his way to his car and the waiting Miguel. He'd call or text to let her know when he'd be home, and if he was going to be too late to see Paola before bedtime, he'd phone to speak to her. When he did return, he immediately shed his business skin for his daughter: playing, chatting, and reading to her until she went to bed. Then he'd go to his study for a while and join Iris for a late supper after he'd completed his work for the day, although he never said anything to her about how it had gone.

One evening, as they companionably cleaned up after dinner, Iris thought she'd broach the subject.

"You don't talk to me about your work like you used to," she said, carefully keeping her eyes focussed on the plate she was washing up.

"I didn't think you'd want me to," he said.

"What made you decide that?"

"I guess I just assumed you wouldn't be interested."

"OK, fair point," she conceded. She waited a beat and asked, "So, how was your day?"

He grinned, one of his really big, easy grins she remembered so well from when they were together. She felt a surprising pang of sadness at what she'd lost.

"It was good, I've had a difficult deal to work through, but it all seems to be coming together now."

Unable to help herself, she blurted out, "So does that mean we can go back to England soon?" She immediately regretted saying it as Sergio's face darkened.

"Ah, that's why you're so anxious to hear about my work."

"No . . ." she trailed off weakly.

"Once this deal is completed then yes, hopefully I shall be in a position to go back to England. I'll do my best to finish things up quickly."

"So how long do you expect us to stay here?" She knew it was probably a good idea to end this topic, but now that she'd actually got him onto the subject of going home, she was determined to get as much information from him as possible.

"As long as I need to stay here," he answered curtly.

"Have you any idea how long that will be?"

"No."

"Don't you think that's a little unreasonable?" she said, far past the point of being able to restrain herself and irritated by Sergio's apparent inability to understand her side of things.

"No, not particularly," he countered. "You have a lovely place to stay, good food, people to help you with Paola whenever you want. What do you have to complain about?"

"I want to go back to London."

"Why? There's nothing for you there."

"It's my home. Our lives are there."

"You're being awkward."

"I am not!"

"Yes, you are. We have discussed this all before. There is no need for you to be in London. You are even able to do your precious work here. There is no problem."

"What about my flat? I'm paying rent and I'm not living in it."

"I will pay your rent," Sergio replied simply.

"Sergio, money isn't always the answer: my things are in my flat, it's my home."

"I will have your things collected and brought here," he said calmly.

"You're not listening to me!" she said, completely exasperated. How could she get through to this man?

"I am listening to you, I just really don't see your difficulties."

"My 'difficulties' are that I am an adult. I have a life. I have a home. I cannot give up my independence and live in a few rooms in your apartment!"

There was silence while he digested this statement. Finally, he replied, "So, you want more space?"

Iris felt like crying with frustration, but stifled her emotions to answer a cool, firm, "No."

"You want me to rent you and Paola a house in Barcelona?" he asked, puzzled.

"No!" she practically screamed. "I don't want your money, your rooms, or your houses. I want my life back! I want to take Paola back to England."

"That is not going to happen," he said flatly, losing the last vestige of the jovial mood he'd exhibited earlier. "Paola is my daughter, and I want her here. If you chose to leave, that's up to you, but she is staying."

"You know that's not going to happen. You're not being fair," she replied quietly.

"Sometimes life isn't fair, in case you hadn't noticed. It isn't fair that I missed out on the first years of my child's life, and she's only just getting to know her father. She stays with me."

And with that he got up and left the room, closing the door firmly behind him as he muttered about having some telephone calls to make.

* * *

Sergio was already in the kitchen when Iris came downstairs the following morning. She'd found it hard to sleep, churning over the argument in her mind, and had woken up early. She blushed as she realised he didn't have anything on under his open dressing gown. Attempting to keep her eyes above waist level, she was distracted by his tanned, muscular chest.

With an embarrassed cough, he drew his robe together. "Bon día," he said gruffly, nodding towards the coffee in what she assumed was an invitation for her to help herself.

She wondered whether he would bring up the argument, but he seemed content to act as if nothing had happened. Evidently he didn't feel the need to carry on the discussion; it was annoying, but, at the same time, fighting with Sergio was exhausting, and she really wasn't up for round two.

He went back to his newspaper and croissant, Iris felt she was intruding upon his private time. She poured herself a coffee and glanced at the open box of delicious-smelling croissants on the counter. He noticed her hesitation, "Help yourself," he said.

Stretching up to get a plate from the cupboard, she was sure she could sense Sergio's eyes on her, although when she turned round he appeared to be completely focussed on his paper.

"Is Paola awake yet?"

"Not when I checked a few minutes ago."

Back to silence. She took a sip of coffee and a bite of buttery croissant. She was reaching for one of the newspaper supplements when Sergio announced: "I have an important work dinner tonight. I would like you to come."

"Me? Why?"

"Because I need a woman to accompany me. You are a woman, yes?"

"Yes, I am. But I'm not going with you," she said, diligently concentrating on her breakfast.

He sighed. It was the exasperated sigh he tended to use whenever she said or did something which wasn't to his liking.

"Nothing's ever simple with you, is it?"

"I'm not the problem," she said, getting up, "You see yourself as the centre of the world and everything has to revolve around your wishes! Well it doesn't!"

I won't be treated like a doll, she thought to herself bitterly, abandoning her breakfast in favour of the solitude of her study.

A quarter of an hour passed before Iris heard footsteps coming up the stairs, and a light tap on the door: "Do you want your breakfast?" Sergio asked, a trace of amusement evident in his voice.

"No, I'm not hungry," she replied, but was betrayed by an untimely rumble from her stomach. She knew she was behaving like a sulky child, but she honestly had no idea how else to deal with Sergio.

He didn't reply. She heard him go along the corridor and open the door to Paola's room. Getting up to check everything was alright, and irritated he was going into Paola's room when she was asleep, she heard Sergio saying, "Hello, my lovely girl, and how did you dream?" Paola chattered away delightedly in reply. Her daughter was well and truly awake and ready to start the day.

"Do you need a hand?" she called out, not wishing to spoil their fun, but also not wanting Sergio to be stuck changing a nappy and making breakfast if he didn't want to.

"No, thank you, we're fine," he answered.

She turned back to the computer screen, but kept one ear listening out. It proved hard to concentrate though, as the sounds of a happy rumpus drifted through the walls. She heard Sergio ask Paola if she'd like something to eat; presumably the answer was in the affirmative because the ruckus soon moved down the hall, Sergio pretending to be the galloping horse and Paola his chivvying jockey.

She couldn't go get her breakfast now, even though she was still famished and dying for a drink. She didn't want Sergio to think she was watching his every move with Paola, and she'd already claimed she wasn't hungry. Not to mention, she was still put out about their argument and had no particular desire to be around him. But, be that as it may, she would have loved to watch them play.

After what seemed like an absolute age, Sergio called out, "We're just off to the shops, is that alright?"

"It's fine," she replied, and she eagerly awaited the sound of the lift doors closing behind them. Restraining herself for several minutes to ensure they weren't merely popping out for a moment or two, she judged the coast was clear and thought she could now safely go down to the kitchen and resume her breakfast. Opening her door, she checked down the corridor and slipped out stealthily — only to step on the coffee and croissant Sergio had brought up for her.

* * *

Iris joined Sergio and Paola downstairs when they got back. Sergio had bought popcorn and ice-cream, and suggested that, as it was raining, they watch a DVD together. They put on 'Toy Story'. Paola didn't last very long in front of the television, and soon began playing with some toys, but Iris and Sergio enjoyed the cartoon, even laughing at the same parts. With each shared chuckle Iris found herself dropping her guard, only to instantly recant, withdrawing back inside her fortress. She suspected it was only a matter of time before he brought up the work dinner again, he was almost certainly trying to butter her up so she'd agree to go with him. She didn't know why he just couldn't find someone else — there were many, many women would love to be his date. He probably only wanted her to come because he knew she didn't want to.

It wasn't until Paola's bath time that he broached the subject again. Well, partially at least.

He glanced at his watch.

"Iris, would you mind doing Paola's stories? I must get ready." Turning to Paola he added, "Papa has to go to a very boring dinner tonight, my darling."

Iris waited for him to either ask her to come again, or more likely, demand that she attend, and she prepared her indignant response. But he said nothing more.

With Paola out of the bath and being read to in bed, he went to get changed. He returned in a tuxedo to give his daughter a goodnight kiss. He looked absolutely ravishing. Iris blushed when he brushed against her as he bent down to kiss the little girl. His scent was intoxicating — he smelt warm and sun-kissed, and it was all Iris could do to keep her hands away from him.

She was ready to reject Sergio's demands again, determined to hold her ground, despite her sudden and irrational longing to be swept off her feet and spend the evening being wined and dined by him. His easy, "See you tomorrow," as he left was deflating.

When would her body stop betraying her like this? But then, it wasn't just her body, her mind was thinking some pretty lustful thoughts about Sergio too. Surely at some point, they must catch up with her heart and realise, after all the hurt he'd caused her, he was most definitely not the right man for her.

* * *

Awoken by sounds in the apartment, Iris checked the time: it was just past three. Realising Sergio had finally returned, she rolled over to go back to sleep, but she heard voices downstairs. Two voices. One was undoubtedly Sergio's, but the other was female. Ah well, Iris thought to herself despondently, it doesn't look like he had too much trouble finding a date, does it? She heard them move into the kitchen, and the quiet conversation continued. Iris put a pillow over her head and forced herself to concentrate on going back to sleep.

* * *

The next morning, Iris struggled to keep Paola as quiet as possible, trying to convince the little girl to creep along the hall like a mouse. Not wanting to disturb Sergio and his lover or to have her daughter confused by seeing her father and his new girlfriend together, she hurried Paola past his room and downstairs into the kitchen for breakfast.

Preparing Paola's breakfast, Iris heard people coming down the stairs and going to the elevator. She turned the radio up: she had absolutely no desire to know what Sergio and his new girlfriend's lovey-dovey parting words were.

"You're down early," said Iris when Sergio came into the kitchen.

"Not really," he replied, looking confused.

Iris fiddled around for longer than necessary making her cup of coffee, so she had something to do with her hands. She stole a glance at him as he opened the fridge. For someone she assumed had been up most of the night, he looked surprisingly good.

"Has your date left?" she asked, trying to sound carefree.

"Yes."

"Did you have a good evening?"

"Yes, thank you," he said amiably.

"You're certainly looking very pleased with yourself," she said, hoping to elicit a response, though further details were really the last thing she wanted, but she just couldn't help herself.

He seemed startled by her change of tack. "Do I?"

"Yes," she confirmed, being careful to avoid eye contact.

"Is this a touch of jealousy I see here?" he teased.

"Of course not! Who you choose to spend your time with is nothing to do with me."

"That's true."

"Although you do need to be careful now that you have Paola around, she might get confused."

"It wasn't a date, and anyway, what did you expect me to do? I needed someone to accompany me, you said no. I found somebody suitable who said yes."

"Suitable? You mean you chose her because she's beautiful?" she asked after a pause.

"No, I chose her because she was available yesterday evening."

"And beautiful."

"What is it with 'beautiful'? You didn't meet her, she's nothing to you."

"Do you think she's beautiful?"

"She's a very lovely person."

"So you did ask her because she's beautiful," declared Iris, not really wanting to think about why she was being so difficult, but determined not to give up until she got the answer she was waiting for.

"So what if I did? I enjoy beautiful things."

"Women are not things," she replied indignantly.

He chose to ignore this comment. Taking a moment, he said steadily, "I'm not going to argue with you about this. There is nothing to argue about. I invited her because she is nice and very good at conversation. People like her."

"I bet they do," Iris said under her breath, returning her attention to Paola.

* * *

It wasn't until the afternoon that Iris walked past one of the guest bedrooms and saw the bed had been slept in. Puzzled, she stopped by the door for a moment.

She hadn't heard Sergio come up behind her, and jumped when he spoke:

"Are you checking how tidy my 'date' left her room?"

"No!" Iris spluttered, her cheeks flushing.

She felt her body stiffen as he turned her gently to face him and said softly, "My date was Carmen, my secretary. I didn't want her travelling home late. She slept in there, by herself."

He stared into her eyes for a moment, as if trying to assess her reaction, before continuing on to his study.

She stayed rooted to the spot, a small smile settling on her lips, despite herself. Life would certainly be a lot easier if she didn't feel this way, but at the moment she couldn't think about that too closely, she was just really glad Sergio had slept alone in his own bed last night!

* * *

Iris put her mobile back down on the desk and sighed. She hardly ever had to go to her company's offices for a meeting, but it was just typical that her boss needed to see her when she was away in another country. She didn't think Sergio would be thrilled when she told him that she and Paola would need to return to the UK in a couple of days. He seemed completely settled in Barcelona, and apparently had no desire or need to go back to London soon himself.

As she wondered how to explain the situation to Sergio in a way that wouldn't involve him completely hitting the roof, she surprised herself by realising she wasn't nearly as keen to fly home as she thought she'd be. In fact, the thought of grey skies and her tiny flat left a feeling of dread in the pit of her stomach.

She knew she'd miss the Spanish sun, her beautiful study, Consuela's wonderful food, and, she admitted to herself, her chats in the evenings with Sergio. It would be pretty hard to readjust to London life again.

She could hardly believe her attitude, especially after how cross she'd been about having to come to Spain in the first place. Now she felt quite settled in Barcelona, and was beginning to enjoy the city. It was a wonderful place to explore, and everywhere seemed so child-friendly. She also had far more support here with Paola than she did in London. In fact, as much as it pained her to admit it, Sergio had been right when he'd said there really wasn't very much for her to return to in London.

That night, Iris waited until their daughter was in bed before approaching Sergio and bringing up her need to leave. The cowardly part of her would have liked to have left it longer, but she had to book a flight for her and

Paola. Unexpectedly, he didn't argue but listened thoughtfully to what she had to say.

"So, it's just one meeting?" he checked.

"Yes," she admitted, determined this time to be honest about her job. "But apparently it's essential I attend."

"Well, you can be gone just for one night, then!" he concluded. "If your meeting is on Thursday, fly to London Wednesday evening. Stay the night in your flat. That way you can check everything is okay, and pick up anything you need. Then go to your meeting the next day and fly back here afterwards."

She was well aware that Sergio was once again taking over and arranging her life, yet was surprised to find she didn't mind. He was being supportive of her work, and trying to make things easier for her.

She was also relieved that he hadn't been angry; she'd anticipated a huge argument and her ending up resigning or something silly like that. This way she could do what she had to in England, and then fly back to the sun.

"That'll be exhausting for Paola," realised Iris, coming down to earth with a bump. Her little girl would find so much travelling in such a short amount of time just too tiring.

"She can stay here," he said decisively. "There's no need for her to fly to London, only for her to come back here again the next day. She doesn't have a meeting."

"But who'll look after her?' Iris asked, thinking first of the practicalities, "It would be too much for Consuela to watch her for so long."

"I'll do it," replied Sergio, as if that should have been perfectly clear from the start.

"You'll be at work."

"I'll take a couple of days off."

Iris was left at a complete loss. Gathering her thoughts, she wondered how he'd manage — as hands-on as he'd become, he'd never had the responsibility of being in charge of the day-to-day business of caring for a toddler, of being constantly on call, and not even able to go for a wee without a tiny person following you. He'd never so much as given Paola a bath without Iris in the house, let alone looked after her by himself overnight.

And apart from this, she and Paola had never spent a night apart: how would Paola feel without her? What if Paola wasn't well, or got upset because her mummy wasn't there?

There also remained the receding, but persistent, niggling unease in her mind that Sergio was certainly capable of disappearing with Paola if he felt it necessary: he'd basically threatened to do so before. Yet surely she hadn't given him any cause to take Paola?

Seeing her concern and sensing all the thoughts whirling through her mind, Sergio put his hands on Iris's shoulders and looked her in the eyes, "We'll be fine. And any problems, Consuela will be here to give a hand. I'm her father. You can trust me."

Funnily enough, hearing these words made Iris finally begin to feel that she could.

* * *

Sergio left work early on the Wednesday, and Iris was packed and ready when he got back to the house. Now it was time to go, she hated the thought of leaving Paola in Spain, even if only for the one night. But it was pointless to work herself up into a state: her meeting was the next morning and the flights were booked, there was no changing her mind now.

Anyway, she'd feel bad if she pulled out. Sergio had had Carmen organise everything, and was insisting he pay Iris's costs. "It's my fault you need to travel all this way," he'd pointed out. He hadn't made a big deal about taking time off work, but she knew from telephone conversations she'd overheard that a lot of rearranging of his own appointments had gone on.

She was grateful to him for going to such an effort so she could go to her meeting, which she realised was nowhere near as important, in the sense of what was at stake, as the meetings he went to every day. It made her feel very valued.

She was ready when Miguel arrived to drive her to the airport. She picked up Paola and gave her a last kiss and a big hug, promising to be back the next day. Then she faced Sergio to say her goodbyes. He leant forward and kissed her on both cheeks.

"Hurry home," he said softly, as if only just realising the task ahead of him. "We'll be anxious to have you back with us."

* * *

Without a toddler in tow, Iris found she really enjoyed the flight to England. Sergio had naturally insisted upon sending her first class, and she felt very naughty relaxing in luxury, with a glass of champagne in her hand.

She idly wondered why she'd had to go to this meeting: her boss hadn't given her a proper reason, nor asked her to prepare anything in particular. Usually most things to do with work could be dealt with over the phone or by email. She was curious, but not concerned. She always did a good job; there was no cause to think the meeting was anything particularly out of the ordinary.

As soon as she got to her flat, she called Sergio. He seemed pleased to hear from her and put Paola on the phone to talk. They sounded like they were having a lovely evening.

It certainly felt peculiar to be back in her old place without Paola: it was so empty. She noticed the damp patch on the bathroom ceiling had grown a bit, but apart from that, the flat was unchanged.

Not having any food in, she ordered a takeaway to watch in front of the television. It fell far below the standard of Consuela's cooking, but it was nice to be able to unwind and only have herself to think about, for a change. She snuggled down under a blanket, feeling the cold after the warmth of Spain.

* * *

Iris watched the clouds drifting by as she ate her sandwich in the park. Well, that was unexpected, she mused. Her meeting had been short and to the point: they'd offered her a promotion when her superior retired in a few months' time. A promotion that would make a real financial difference to her and Paola's lives. The catch was that she'd have to work longer hours, and not completely from home as she did now. It would involve a fair amount of rearranging her life, given the childcare she'd need. What was the right thing to do? Obviously she wanted to be the best mother she could be for Paola. But would earning more money make her a better mother if it meant not being able to spend as much time with her little girl as she did now.

Maybe she'd be able to afford some of those things Sergio considered so important for a child to have. She knew he'd happily buy anything at all for Paola, he'd made that perfectly clear, but she didn't like to be beholden to him. Despite all their difficulties, and his demands, his being a part of Paola's life was proving far better than expected. Yet, she was so used to providing for her daughter, she was still finding it hard to let go.

* * *

Not wanting to disturb Sergio too early, she had texted to check everything was okay, before her meeting. It was only now, with everything wrapped up and with some time to fill until her flight back to Barcelona, that she realised he hadn't texted back. She tried to call him, but her mobile didn't have any signal. She considered using a payphone, but sternly told herself to stop being such a worrywart. She'd be seeing Paola in only a few hours. She was fine.

Instead of worrying about nothing, she should be enjoying a few child-free hours in London. She could do some window-shopping, go to the cinema, have a nice meal . . . But all she really wanted to do was get back to Spain, to see Paola and Sergio and find out how they'd got along without her. She was sure they'd have had a brilliant time, but hoped Paola would be pleased to see her.

At the airport, Iris tried again to call, but her phone refused to connect her. It was a cheap old thing, she really needed to replace it when she had the money. Sergio probably had texted her back, but her rubbish phone hadn't received it yet, no doubt it would once she was back in Barcelona.

* * *

Iris was tired after her long day, and pleased to see Miguel waiting for her after she'd been through customs. She was disappointed Sergio and Paola hadn't come to meet her, but knew she was being silly — her flight could have easily been delayed and it would have been pointless for Sergio to have had Paola waiting around in a busy airport. After all, she'd only been gone one night, even though it felt like longer. She was looking forward to discussing the promotion with Sergio and getting his thoughts on whether she should accept the offer. She trusted his judgment, when it came to business at least, and knew he'd give her good advice.

"Hola, Miguel," Iris called out cheerfully.

"Hola, señora. Your flight, it was good?"

"Yes, thanks. How's Paola?"

"I do not know. The house was very quiet this morning. I did not see Paola or Senor Batista-Sanchez."

Despite her very best intentions, Iris couldn't help beginning to panic slightly at the news. Obviously Sergio and Paola could just have gone out somewhere together. They could have popped out to the local park for an hour or so. But then again . . . the last couple of days would have been the ideal opportunity for Sergio to disappear with Paola. Iris had been gone for over twenty-four hours; he could have got Paola a very long way away if he'd wanted to.

Miguel was eager to chat, he loved any opportunity to practise his English. She answered his questions as politely as she could, but she was rather preoccupied — though aware she was overreacting, she couldn't quite vanquish her feelings of unease. The last thing she wanted to do was talk about the weather.

It seemed like forever until they reached the apartment. Iris quickly thanked Miguel and hurried inside. Downstairs was quiet and tidy: the lack of any toys on the floor a sure sign Paola had not been playing there.

Iris went upstairs, calling for Paola, and almost collided with an absolutely exhausted-looking, unshaven, Sergio.

Chapter 6

"Shh," Sergio said gently, "Paola's sleeping."

"What's she doing in bed now?" Iris whispered back, checking her watch. "She should have been up from her nap over two hours ago. I'll never be able to get her to sleep tonight!"

"She's been unwell," Sergio answered, rubbing his eyes. "I was up most of the night with her. She's got chicken pox. I called the doctor out in the early hours, he wasn't too pleased."

"Chicken pox?" she said. "She was fine when I left!"

"I know. After I'd spoken to you, I ran her bath and noticed some spots on her tummy. She seemed happy, and Consuela knew what it was immediately. She said Paola needed rest and plenty to drink."

He tiredly ran his hand through his hair, taking a moment to collect his thoughts.

"I didn't want to worry you, you were so far away and couldn't do anything, Paola was fine then, there didn't seem any point in calling," he said plaintively, clearly thinking she would be cross with him.

"It was only later when Consuela was leaving for the night, that I heard Paola crying. She was burning hot and very upset. I gave her infant paracetamol, but it didn't help, so I called the doctor."

"Poor Paola! And poor you!"

"I've been trying to call you today, but I couldn't get through," he continued apologetically.

"Sorry about that. My stupid phone seems to have finally died," she explained. "I'll go and check on Paola."

"Don't worry, I won't wake her," she added in response to the look of despair instantly clouding Sergio's face.

"Would you like a coffee?" he asked.

"Yes, thanks, I'll be back down in five minutes."

She crept into Paola's darkened room and made her way to the bed, stepping over the various toys that littered the floor.

Covered in angry red spots, all dutifully dabbed with pink calamine lotion, Paola looked like a different child to the healthy, tanned little girl Iris had left only the day before. She looked pale, but comfortable. As she was in a nice, deep sleep, Iris ventured a gentle touch on her daughter's forehead. She didn't feel hot.

Satisfied that Paola was alright, Iris went downstairs to find Sergio. She discovered her abandoned bag in the hallway. Miguel must have brought it in from the car, but hearing them talking at the top of the stairs, hadn't wanted to disturb them and so had left it in the hall.

Joining Sergio in the kitchen, she again noticed how tired and worried he looked. This was definitely not the Sergio she was used to. Glancing up as she came in, his anxious face spoke volumes.

"She's fast asleep," she reassured him, "And her temperature's gone."

"That's good," he said with a nod. "The doctor was here again, maybe three hours ago. He was pleased with how she'd improved."

She took the coffee Sergio offered her, "Did you put the calamine lotion on?"

"Yes, Consuela got it for me as soon as the chemist opened this morning."

"You're really tired," Iris said gently.

"I'm okay," he replied, rubbing his eyes. "My back's a bit stiff. I slept on her floor last night."

"Thanks for looking after her so well."

He was silent for a moment, then commented quietly, "I hate her being ill."

"I know what you mean."

"I don't think I ever really considered how hard it must have been for you sometimes, looking after Paola on your own."

"It wasn't always easy," she admitted, "But she's more than worth the tough times."

He nodded his head. "I don't think the doctor appreciated having to leave his bed," he said, changing the subject with a tired smile.

"I doubt he did, but you were concerned, and you did what you thought best."

He looked down at his drink, clearly recalling the previous night.

"She'll be better before you know it."

Sergio gave her a small smile.

"Where's Consuela?" Iris asked, realising she hadn't seen the housekeeper since she'd come back. Usually by now she'd be busily preparing Paola's tea.

"She insisted on staying here last night in one of the spare bedrooms in case Paola or I needed her. I sent her home after she'd been to the chemist for me this morning. I told her to take the rest of the day off. She didn't want to go, I had to promise to keep her updated on Paola."

Hearing Paola call out, "Mama," they both jumped up and hurried upstairs to Paola's bedroom. They found their daughter awake and sitting up in bed. She was pale, but clearly pleased to see her mum back.

"I'm hungry," Paola declared.

Iris walked over and picked her up for a cuddle, again checking the temperature of the little girl's forehead with the back of her hand. She still felt cool.

Iris carried Paola downstairs to the kitchen. Paola sat on her lap, obviously a lot better, and enjoying being the centre of attention as she snuggled up to her mother and watched Sergio prepare a some toast and a drink for her.

"There you go, my angel, it is good to see you wanting to eat again," he said, passing Paola her plate and kissing her on the head.

Once Paola had polished off every crumb, she was tucked up on the sofa in Sergio's smaller sitting room to watch some cartoons.

Iris suggested Sergio go upstairs for an hour's siesta, being very careful to avoid the word "nap," knowing that would turn him off the idea straight away. He declined her offer, but said he'd sit down with Paola, he had some papers he needed to go through.

Having gone to get them another drink, Iris returned to find Sergio fast asleep next to his daughter, his papers scattered on the floor where they'd fallen off his lap.

Kneeling down, Iris picked up his work and put it on the antique coffee table in front of him, along with his tea for when he woke up, although judging from his snoring she doubted he would anytime soon. Each of his funny little snores was greeted by a corresponding giggle from Paola.

Iris sat on the other side of her daughter, relieved she seemed to be over the worst of her illness. As a father, Sergio had gone up another big notch in her estimation — he'd done exactly what she would have in the same situation. Except maybe calling the private doctor out: if Iris was ever worried about Paola's health out-of-hours, it meant a trip to the nearest Accident and Emergency Department. This is how the other half lives, she thought to herself wryly, looking around her at the spacious and exquisitely furnished apartment, and realising she was rapidly becoming very used to living as the other half did. Maybe Sergio was right — money was important. It certainly made life an awful lot easier. But did that mean she should accept the promotion she was being offered at work? She couldn't decide.

Speaking to Sergio about it later that evening didn't make things any clearer — his enigmatic response had puzzled her, as had the fact that, for once, he'd seemed determined to keep his opinions to himself, "You need to do what is right for you, Iris. But there's no need to rush and make your decision yet. They said to take as long as you need to decide. Wait a little, and then see how you feel."

Sergio spent the night on the floor of Paola's bedroom again and Iris wasn't in the least bit surprised when he made no mention of going into work the next morning. He stayed at home and, rather than disappearing up to his office, set his laptop up in the sitting room. Paola played quietly and watched television, chatting away happily to her daddy. Iris worried he wouldn't be able to get much done, but he didn't seem too concerned, and from the few quick phone calls he made, it was clear he was delegating as much as possible.

When Iris went up to her room later that afternoon, she found a parcel on her bed, with a note in Sergio's handwriting reading, "For you Mama, so that Papa and I can always speak to you. Love Paola." Excitedly unwrapping the gift, Iris discovered a new mobile phone, all charged and set up. The background wallpaper was a photo of Iris, Sergio, and Paola together, taken the day they'd gone to the zoo; they looked like a very happy family.

* * *

As much as Iris hated feeling like she was under Sergio's control, on some level she had a lot more freedom, should she choose to accept it, than she'd had in London.

Consuela was always delighted to babysit Paola, and her little girl was obviously flourishing: a naturally shy child, she was becoming far more confident and her beautiful smile never seemed to leave her face. Her laughter could always be heard ringing happily throughout the apartment.

Iris's previous worries about Paola being lonely here in Barcelona had been firmly extinguished. She was picking up both Catalan and Spanish amazingly quickly and had made friends at the new playgroup she'd started at for a couple of mornings a week. She was developing quite the social life.

In truth, Iris was also settling in well to life in Spain. It was nice to have people around the house to talk to. The sunshine naturally lifted her spirits, and knowing there was backup should something happen to Paola made her more relaxed. And she couldn't deny that the money-worry-free cocoon Sergio had wrapped her in was rather comfortable. Bumping into him unexpectedly that day in the park, despite the stress and chaos it had caused, had been cathartic, and meant an end to the niggling worry and feelings of guilt she'd felt whenever she thought of what she'd hidden from him and of their daughter growing up fatherless. She was amazed things were actually better now that her long-protected secret was out.

* * *

Iris was surprised at Sergio's manner when she came downstairs for breakfast with a fully-recovered Paola, a couple of weeks after her London trip. He seemed agitated and fretful. It was early, so Consuela wasn't in yet, but there was a box of fresh pastries on the table. Presumably he'd already been out, and had picked them up from the bakery a couple of streets away.

Paola immediately climbed up on a chair to investigate the box, bringing a smile to her father's serious face. As Sergio and Iris stiltedly chatted, she got the feeling there was something he wanted to speak to her about, and was building up the courage.

She waited patiently while he gave Paola a drink and a pain au chocolat and then offered her one. Clearly he was trying to butter her up before asking a favour. Was he going to ask her to tag along with him on some business dinner again?

It was only after Paola had finished eating and had got down from the table to play, that Sergio finally got around to explaining what he wanted.

"I need to visit my mother. She lives a couple of hours drive from here, I thought I'd go for a week or so. I want her to meet Paola." Before she could reply, Sergio added, "I would also like her to meet you, but I understand if you choose not to come."

As irritating as it was to have Sergio dictating what she and Paola needed to do, yet again, for once she decided not to argue. Sergio's mother was Paola's grandmother, of course they should get to know each other. Her trip back to London had shown her that there was no desperate need to return there, and she certainly had no urge to do so at the moment. Also, to be honest, she was more than a little curious to meet Sergio's family.

He looked stunned when she breezily answered, "Sure, that's a lovely idea, it's important Paola meets your family. When would you like to go?"

"Er, I've got a few things at work that I need to finish up with, but I should be done by tomorrow evening. Shall we leave Wednesday?" he asked tentatively. He seemed anxious not to rock the boat in case she suddenly changed her mind.

"That sounds fine."

"Wonderful," he said. "I won't be taking any work with me, but please bring anything you need to work on, although I should warn you the house is rather remote, there's no internet connection."

"You're not going to work, or even check your email for a week?" she said incredulously.

"My mother likes me to relax when I am with her, she can be rather strict about it," he replied with a smile. "But I do know a few places I can drive to nearby 'on errands' where I can get online."

"I can't wait to meet this woman who has so much power over you," said Iris with a laugh.

"I think my mother feels the same way," muttered Sergio, as he got up from the table and went to get ready for work.

* * *

On Wednesday another beautiful day. The heat was already building as Miguel packed their luggage into the back of a large Range Rover. Sergio again was not quite his usual confident self. He paced around, checking his watch frequently, as if it were terribly important that they leave exactly on time. His agitation rubbed off on Iris, and made her anxious, she checked the bags at least twice, worried that she'd forgotten something essential.

They didn't talk much to each other for the first part of the drive. Paola kept up a steady stream of pleasant jabber about which toys and books she'd brought for the journey. Eventually, when Paola had nodded off, Sergio turned towards Iris and said, "My mother is very excited about meeting Paola, and you. I think she's been preparing things for Paola ever since she heard we were coming," he said awkwardly.

"Oh, that's nice," Iris replied, not really sure what else to say. She was certainly curious to meet Sergio's family, but at the moment she was primarily nervous. What if they were all like Sergio? Would they have to take it in turns to boss her around? She let out an involuntary giggle at the thought, and received a puzzled glance from Sergio.

"So, tell me about your family, you don't really talk about them much," she said.

Sergio looked at Iris intently for a moment, checking she really wanted to hear about his family and wasn't just being polite. Deciding her interest was genuine, he replied, "I'm the youngest of five children, and the only boy."

Checking she remained interested, he continued, "My sisters are all married. At last count, I have five nieces and four nephews. They've all stayed here in Spain and visit my mother regularly, much more regularly than I do, I'm afraid. My mother lives in the house we all grew up in. Actually, she grew up there, as well. She's been by herself since my father died."

"When did your father pass away?"

"Three years ago," was his concise reply. He pointed out an old church they were driving past, and began filling her in on some of the history of the area.

Iris knew Sergio was changing the subject, but if he didn't want to talk about his father then she wasn't going to press him. It saddened her though that Sergio didn't feel that he could open up with her, but maybe she was asking too much to expect this from their relationship.

Iris wondered again where exactly they were going: all she knew was that they'd been travelling for a couple of hours and were heading northwards along rougher and rougher roads, they seemed to be in the middle of nowhere. The hot summer had made the arid landscape dusty and tired-looking, and they kept the windows of the 4x4 firmly closed and the air conditioning high. Paola slept contentedly between her mother and father.

Finally they turned off the road and drove down what seemed to be barely more than a dirt track. Tall, mature holly oaks lined either side of the lane, casting delightful cool shade all around. Soon it became clear that the track was a driveway, leading to a large, white stone villa. Built in the traditional style of the area, the grand house was complete with a veranda and balconies.

Miguel parked the Range Rover and Iris climbed out, grateful to stretch her legs. Paola was still fast asleep. Iris leant back into the car and unbuckled her daughter's seatbelt and gently lifted her up. The little girl was in such a deep slumber she barely stirred.

"Would you like me to take her?" Sergio asked.

"No thanks, we'll be fine." She carried Paola towards the house, a small knot of nerves forming in her stomach. Keeping her daughter with her both calmed her and provided an outlet of displacement activity. What was her reception going to be like? She had after all kept this woman's grandchild from her for the last two years. When she'd brought up the subject back in Barcelona, Sergio had tried to reassure her, promising his mother bore her no ill will, but she wasn't certain his words weren't largely motivated by self-interest. In-laws could be hard to manage even in a conventional relationship, and hers was anything but.

Standing in the doorway of the villa was a slim, tiny woman with shoulder-length black hair. She was casually but elegantly dressed in beige linen trousers and a fitted white shirt. It was only when Iris got closer that the lines on the woman's face betrayed her age. She assumed this was Sergio's mother. She reminded Iris of a small bird, and looked like a strong wind could blow her away. Iris couldn't believe that this delicate person had given birth to five children!

Sergio walked over and hugged his mother. When they broke apart, he was firmly held at arm's-length and thoroughly examined. Presumably satisfied by what she saw, she patted his stomach and announced happily in halting English, "You are well!", then peered eagerly around her son towards Iris and Paola. Sergio turned to follow her gaze and smiled warmly. Paola looked lovely, and Iris knew he was proud and thrilled to be introducing her to his mother.

Under the old lady's quiet scrutiny, Iris blushed, but held her ground, waiting for Sergio's mother to complete her assessment. She could see that Sergio had inherited his mother's eyes, but right now she only hoped he got his quick temper from his father. Sensing no hostility, Iris ventured a tentative smile, and it was instantly reciprocated. Feeling as if she'd passed the test, she relaxed, and handed Paola to Sergio, so he could present her to her grandmother.

Introducing Paola, Sergio spoke quietly in Catalan to his mother, and Paola shyly peeped with big eyes from behind her teddy bear.

"How beautiful you are," his mother said with a heavy Spanish accent, reaching out to gently stroke her granddaughter's hair. The little girl giggled and held her bear out for inspection.

She cooed appreciatively, examining the teddy and explaining to Paola, "I am your grandmother, your àvia. Can you say àvia?"

Paola just giggled shyly again and Sergio motioned to Iris to come forward, "Iris, this is my mother, Maria. Mama, Iris."

Maria kissed Iris warmly on both cheeks, and enveloped her in a hug.

Sergio and his mother again reverted to Catalan. They spoke rapidly to each other, for what seemed like a long time, with Sergio occasionally glancing across at Iris, checking she was alright. Maria too consulted her face every now and again as if trying to gauge her reaction to what was being said, but Iris's minimal grasp of the language meant she had no hope of following the fluid conversation, although she was in no doubt that at least some of it was about her.

At length, Sergio and his mother appeared to reach an agreement. Turning to Iris he said apologetically, "Sorry to throw you in the deep end, but my mother has organised a welcome dinner for us this evening. She's invited my sisters and their families."

"Oh, um . . . it'll be lovely to meet everyone," Iris replied.

"She wonders if you would like to see your room and freshen up before people get here?"

"Yes, please. It was a long journey, I could do with getting Paola unpacked and changed," she said with relief, glad to have the excuse to hide away for a bit and collect her thoughts.

Sergio, Iris, and Paola followed Maria up the stairs. At the top, she turned left and opened the door to a beautiful small room, sunny and airy, painted pale yellow and with a dark, polished hardwood floor. Inside was an intricately carved wooden child's bed, matching chest of drawers with a changing mat all ready, and a dainty antique wardrobe. Dotted around were various old toys. Sergio wandered over to a rather battered soft rabbit and picked it up, a smile playing on his lips. Showing it to his mother, she smiled back, answering quietly in Catalan.

"He was mine," he explained to Iris, "I did not realise my mother had kept him."

Iris thought it was touching to hear the rabbit referred to as "he" rather than "it." Though when Sergio handed him to Paola, she didn't seem too impressed and dropped it unceremoniously on the floor. Iris picked him up and put him carefully back on the bed.

Maria gestured towards another door next to the wardrobe, and led them all out of Paola's room into an adjoining bedroom, as charmingly decorated and furnished as the first, but with an en-suite shower-room.

Kissing Iris gently on the cheek, Maria left her to settle in, and was followed out by Sergio with Paola in tow, she was excited to see the rest of the house.

Iris stood and then slowly spun round, taking in the room. Finding herself drawn to the huge window framed by olive green shutters, she walked over and took in the villa's gorgeous gardens. She couldn't imagine a more tranquil and calming view than the one that greeted her: lovely trees, gently sloping hills, and the glimmer of sea in the distance. Goodness, how lucky was Sergio to grow up in this place?

Her reverie was disturbed by Sergio knocking on the door, and bringing in her suitcase. Paola was "helping."

"Is your room alright?" he asked, looking around, "It used to be my grandmother's."

"It's beautiful," she said. "It must have been amazing growing up here."

"Yes, it was idyllic," he said wistfully

After a pause, he continued, "I'm afraid my mother doesn't speak much English. Let me know if there's anything you need."

"She seems really nice. Very welcoming."

"My mother loves to have her family around her — it means the world to her. She's thrilled to have Paola here."

"Of course she is."

"And you. Mama is so pleased that you've come."

"Ah, I knew you two were gossiping about me!" she replied teasingly.

Sergio hesitated, looking embarrassed and admitted, "Yes. Um, my mother wasn't sure if we'd be sharing a room here. She's rather traditional, and wouldn't normally allow an unmarried couple to share a bed under her roof, but I think she was so anxious to make you feel welcome, she was willing to bend her rules."

"Oh," she said, her cheeks flushing. She didn't really know what else to say.

"Well, I'd better go and have a shower. Do you want to do the same? My mother will happily babysit, if you think Paola will be okay with her."

"Er, yes, thank you, that would be great. I'm sure she'll be fine, I won't be long," Iris said.

"I'll tell my mother to get me if there are any problems. Come on, Paola."

Paola had been handed the rabbit again, but was eyeing it with suspicion. She dropped it and took Sergio's hand. They went out, closing the door behind them.

Iris was pleased to have a moment to herself. She had a shower and re-did her makeup, then dressed in a light, summery dress and strappy sandals. She heard a car pull up just as she was putting her earrings in and giving herself a last once-over in the mirror. She looked, and felt, relaxed and happy. Who would have thought it? If anyone had said to her a few months ago that her life would have taken her here, and that she'd be content with it, she never would have believed them.

Sergio was soon back, "If you're ready," he said, "I figured we could go down together so you don't have to face everyone by yourself."

"Are they that scary?" she asked with a smile.

"Oh yes, far worse than me," he replied with a wink.

* * *

After a couple of days, Iris wondered how she could ever have felt nervous coming to this lovely place. She couldn't remember ever feeling more welcome in somebody's home. From the first day she'd been happily accepted and considered part of the family. She was also pleased with how her Catalan was improving.

One of her biggest surprises was how easy she found being with Sergio's mother. The language barrier seemed to, if not quite slip away, be greatly eased by Maria's patience and thoughtfulness. They spent many hours together in the kitchen thanks to Maria's love of cooking and her desire to share it with Iris. She was always happy to have Iris helping her, and to show her how to make the delicious Catalan dishes she produced for them all.

The rest of Sergio's family dropped by frequently and were just as welcoming. His sisters and their husbands spoke some English, and were keen to improve their skills by chatting to her. The only thing that made Iris uncomfortable was that they were all convinced she and Sergio were a couple; she saw the conspiratorial looks that passed between Sergio's sisters whenever they saw her and

Sergio together. She found all the attention a bit embarrassing, but Sergio didn't seem to mind, and just ignored it, so she endeavoured to do the same.

Iris had never really considered that she'd missed out on anything growing up, but being with Sergio's big loving family made her feel her own childhood might have been lacking something. As an only child growing up with just a rather distant, uninterested mother and not in touch with any extended family, there hadn't been the happy bustle and camaraderie, or reassurance of a large, supportive family. She could just imagine a young Sergio in this amazing villa, playing with his sisters and all his numerous cousins, aunts, and uncles. It was wonderful that Paola would now have that too.

On the third evening there, Iris came downstairs to the kitchen after she'd given Paola her bath. Paola scampered off to play with her cousins in the garden and Maria poured Iris a glass of deep red Rioja.

Handing her another full glass of wine, Maria said, "For Sergio."

"Where is he?" Iris asked.

Maria pointed out towards a large tree in the distance.

"He's there?" checked Iris.

Maria nodded in agreement.

Iris made her way gingerly towards the tree, she couldn't see Sergio anywhere near it. It was only when she got much closer that she spotted the ladder leant against the trunk, leading up into the branches. The tree was green and lush, and in the dusky light, she could just make out the tree house hidden amongst the shadows and leaves.

Iris debated whether or not to climb up, but the two wine glasses she was holding decided matters for her. Instead she called out, "Sergio!" She heard movement, then the creaking of wood, before Sergio's head appeared near what must have been the top of the ladder. "I have a drink for you," she explained. "Your mother sent it and told me where to find you," she added for clarification in case he thought she'd been randomly searching the garden for him.

Sergio reached down from his perch towards the proffered glass with a cheerful, "Gràcies." She stood on her tiptoes and passed the drink to his outstretched hand. His head disappeared from view and Iris was turning to head back to the house, when she heard him shout, "Well, aren't you coming up?"

She climbed the ladder awkwardly, with her wine glass in her left hand, curious to know exactly what he was doing up there. Reaching out, he relieved her of her drink and helped her into what she discovered was a very cosy den. The floor protested at the added weight, groaning ominously, but otherwise seemed fairly sturdy. It was like something out of an Enid Blyton tale with its shutter-clad little windows, and floor covered with blankets and cushions. Once properly inside, Iris closed the thick, round wooden door.

"What are you doing hiding in here?" she asked Sergio. He looked very comfortable and bohemian, sipping his wine and reclining on a pile of cushions.

"This was always my favourite spot to come and think when I was young. It was just about the only place I could get any peace, my sanctuary from my sisters."

She laughed. "Do you ever wish you lived nearer your family?" she found herself asking. "I'm sure you must miss them terribly." As soon as she said it she thought, perhaps not, he always comes across as so self-reliant.

"Sometimes," he admitted with a broad smile, surprising her.

"How often do you manage to visit?" she said, pleased he was finally opening up.

"Whenever I can, which is probably not as frequently as I should."

In comfortable silence, they sipped their drinks and listened to the sound of the stream that ran at the very end of the garden babbling away to itself. When Sergio did speak, it was as though it took him a great deal of courage to do so: "Since my father died, I find it hard to come back here. Everything reminds me of him. When I'm not here, I don't have to think about him so much."

They both quietly processed Sergio's confession. She chose her words very carefully: "I'm sorry about your father. My dad died when I was a baby, I don't remember him at all, but somehow I've always missed him."

He nodded in acknowledgment; he seemed to be concentrating very intently on his wine.

"I know it's upsetting, but it's important for you to be able to think about your father so you can hold onto the memories you have of him. And it must be so good for your mum to see you, you're her baby," she said, smiling.

"This is the first time I've visited since Papa passed away that I haven't wanted to leave pretty much the moment I got here. It's been lovely showing Paola around and seeing her with my family and in this house."

"She certainly likes her cousins," Iris said, catching sight of her daughter out of the window. She could just make out Paola happily running around with two of her new friends, under the watchful eyes of one of her many aunties. "Actually, I should be popping her to bed, it's getting late."

She began to get up, but he stopped her, putting his hand on her arm, "She's happy, don't spoil her fun."

Sitting back down, she locked eyes with him. He suddenly seemed much closer than before. She was acutely aware of how small a space they occupied. It may well have been large enough for him to escape to when he was a child, but there really wasn't a lot of room for two adults to move around without touching.

He tenderly tucked a loose strand of hair behind her ear. Almost as if it were all happening in slow motion, she realised that he was moving in to kiss her. Panicking, she shot to her feet, bumping her head on the roof in the process.

"I'd better go and check if your mum needs any help," she managed to blurt out, scrambling out of the doorway and down the ladder, leaving her wine in the treehouse in her rush. Missing the final rung, she ended up making a rather undignified stumble as she reached the ground. She didn't look back as she half walked, half ran to the safety of the house.

* * *

Sergio carried a very tired Paola into the kitchen about ten minutes later. He passed her to Iris for a good night kiss, saying, "I'll take her up to bed if you're busy here."

"Thanks, that would be great," she replied, being very careful not to make eye contact, concentrating extremely intently on the washing up she was doing.

That was the last Iris saw of him that evening: despite the earliness of the hour, she took herself up to hide in her room not long afterwards. As she lay restlessly in bed, she pondered her reaction to Sergio's advances. Well, she was ninety-nine per cent sure there had been advances and that she hadn't merely imagined him leaning towards her. But then, what if he'd just been shifting his body weight to get more comfortable? If that were the case, thank goodness she hadn't responded and moved in for a kiss! That would have been even more excruciatingly embarrassing than what had actually happened.

Oh, dear me, she thought unhappily, this would all be so much easier if he weren't so horribly attractive.

She was still very wary of his charms because of the way she'd been manipulated that night he'd come for dinner at her flat, when he'd first broached coming to Spain. Perhaps he was up to his old tricks. Did he want something from her? Well, he might be handsome and ever so seductive, but she'd be on the lookout and certainly wasn't about to fall for his games again!

Chapter 7

Still hiding away the following afternoon, Iris was working in her bedroom, when she heard a tap on the door. "Come in," she called out, and turning round she saw Sergio enter the room.

"Is everything alright?" she asked, quickly focussing back on the laptop screen.

"I have an event in Barcelona that I need to attend tomorrow night," he said.

Ah, so here it was — what he'd been after. A ready list of excuses sprung to the forefront of her mind.

Her expression must have warned him that she had anticipated what he was going to say next, and was poised to reject his invitation.

He hurriedly continued, "Carmen, my secretary, is ill. I need to take someone. It's not that much of a sacrifice, is it?"

Did he really think that she was that naive? He'd tried to charm her — thinking she'd swoon like some girl in a Victorian romance, and agree to his every wish — but failed, and then imagined she hadn't even noticed his plan! Well, he could think again. Though furious with him now, she was well aware of her attraction to him and the power he held over her, especially when she'd had a glass of wine. She was determined not to put herself in such a vulnerable position.

"I'm not going to beg you," he said into the silence, "I need a favour and I'm asking you to help me."

"Surely you can find some other woman to go with you."

"Is that really what you want?" he replied, scanning her face, searching for an answer there.

Betraying her best intentions, she sighed quietly. "No," she admitted. Damn him.

A mute battle waged within her: her anger with Sergio remained — he treated her like a plaything he could control by pushing the right buttons. But, despite everything that had gone on between them, she found him very hard to resist, particularly when his deep, brown eyes were so intently concentrated on her.

Something inside her relaxed, letting go of her worries, and before she knew quite what she was getting herself into, she blurted out, "Did you try to kiss me last night, in the treehouse?"

"Yes," he said immediately, "And I was hoping for a slightly more favourable reaction from you than the one I received."

"But, Sergio, don't you see that you can't just pretend to want to kiss me so I'll agree to go to some dinner thing you need a date for? You're not being fair!"

Sergio looked mystified.

"I wasn't pretending," he said simply.

"Sorry?"

"I wasn't pretending," he repeated, then clarified, "I wanted to kiss you."

"Oh," she said.

A long, embarrassed silence swallowed the conversation. Neither of them knew quite how to respond. Sergio finally ventured a cough and a tentative, "So, will you come with me?"

A tad sheepishly, she mumbled, "I don't have anything to wear."

"Don't worry, I'll organise everything."

Suddenly feeling very shy, she nodded and pretended to go back to work.

"Bueno," he said, "We'll leave at nine tomorrow morning."

"Nine a.m.?" she said, looking up from her screen in surprise. "For an evening event?"

"It'll take a while to get back to the city, and we'll need to get ready. We'll stay the night in my apartment and drive back here Sunday morning."

"What about Paola?"

"Paola will have people fighting to take care of her. She'll be fine and will have a wonderful weekend."

She knew he was right, and strangely she already trusted Maria enough to leave Paola with her — after all, she'd brought up five children of her own! She found it difficult to let people into her and Paola's world, but she was learning to let go. Besides, it was only for one night — with all her cousins around to occupy her, Paola would hardly have a chance to miss her.

* * *

At five to nine the following morning, Miguel drew up outside the house in Sergio's Range Rover. Knowing by now they'd be leaving precisely on time, Iris had already brought her bag downstairs and was in the middle of saying her goodbyes to Paola. The little girl smothered her mother and father in kisses and hugs then returned to breakfast with her grandmother.

On the drive to the city, Sergio was friendly and filled Iris in about what they'd be doing that evening. She found herself becoming more and more tense as the details of what she'd let herself in for emerged. It was a charity black-tie dinner and dance, and a major fixture of the Barcelona social calendar. Politicians and celebrities often attended. And, yes, she would be expected to dance. The dinner would be ten courses, cooked by a world-renowned chef. She hated to think how much the tickets must have cost. She'd never been to anything like this, and was worried she'd be well out of her comfort zone. How would she even be able to chat to anyone when they'd all be speaking Spanish or Catalan? And though, in the heat of the moment, she'd agreed to him organising something for her to wear, what if she didn't like it or it didn't fit? She was also nervous about what might happen, following his revelation the previous day. Did he want something more between them? Did she want something to happen? Maybe the best thing would be to just see how things played out.

* * *

When they arrived at the apartment, Iris did her best to get to the bags before Miguel, but once again he moved surprisingly quickly for his age. The poor old man — Sergio really shouldn't work him so hard. She was sure Sergio was deliberately taking his time going inside after Miguel opened the car door for him. It wasn't very nice: yes, Miguel was Sergio's employee, but he was elderly and Sergio should be more caring and understanding. Would it kill him to carry his own bag?

She kept quiet until Miguel was out of earshot, then couldn't resist blurting out, "Why don't you ever help him? It's cruel to make him do so much at his age!"

He gave her a cool look and replied, "And how do you think he'd feel if I stepped in and did his job for him? Miguel is a proud man. He would never agree to work for me if he felt he wasn't needed or was considered next to useless. And then what would he do? He has no family of his own, and has worked for my father's family for as long as anyone can remember. Of course I don't need someone to fetch and carry for me, but Miguel needs me to need him."

Iris felt silly. Why did she always jump to the wrong conclusion when it came to Sergio and his motives? He was constantly proving her assumptions wrong, turning out to be far nicer and more considerate than she gave him credit for.

"I'm sorry," she said. "I didn't realise."

"You seem determined to always believe the worst of me, Iris. Perhaps one day you'll realise I'm really not so bad," he replied gently. "Now, I've got some phone calls to make. If you need me I'll be in my study."

"Um, ok," she said, glad to have been forgiven, but wondering what she was supposed to do with herself for the rest of the day until they went out.

As he went to leave, he paused and mischievously added, "Oh, I nearly forgot. Some people will be here soon to help you get ready for tonight."

He disappeared into his study, closing the door behind him, before she had a chance to question him further. Indeed, she barely had a chance to wonder who on earth was going to turn up, when the doorbell rang and Consuela came bustling out of the kitchen in response. She greeted Iris with a conspiratorial smile and opened the door to two, very smart, middle-aged women, surrounded by boxes, cases and a rail that held one item, completely covered with a mysterious black plastic cover.

They introduced themselves briskly in faultless English, and swiftly set to work.

* * *

At just gone seven, her two fairy godmothers left, leaving Iris transformed. Everything from her eyebrows to her fingernails had been beautified. Her hair had been teased into a 1920s style that worked perfectly with the gorgeous, floor-length sky-blue gown brought by the women. The dress suited Iris's figure perfectly, accentuating her best bits, and giving her curves where she hadn't known she had them. Its elegant layers gave the skirt a very dramatic feel, and made a wonderful swishing noise as she twirled, which Iris couldn't help trying. It had been a long time since she'd got properly scrubbed up, and she'd certainly never worn anything as chic and glamorous as this.

She was in the process of admiring herself in the bedroom mirror when Sergio knocked on the door. Quickly turning away from her reflection, she pretended to be busy fiddling with her new clutch bag, before calling out that he could come in.

"Preciosa!" exclaimed Sergio as he entered and caught sight of her.

"Your secretary has good taste," stuttered a flustered Iris, trying to draw the attention away from herself.

"Carmen?"

"Yes, didn't she pick out the dress?"

"She didn't choose it, I did," he answered. "I'm glad you like it."

"Oh," she said in surprise. "It's beautiful. Thank you so much."

"It was my pleasure," he said, evidently pleased with her reaction.

She smiled appreciatively at him, using the moment to take him in: black tie definitely suited his physique. How could he look even sexier all covered up than when he was wearing a lot less? She felt her cheeks heating up. Tearing her attention away from his body, she noticed his bow tie had settled slightly crookedly. Strangely, it was comforting to see this slight imperfection: he was so capable and good at anything he set his hand to, but here was a small something she could help him with. Stepping closer, she took hold of the tie and did it up expertly.

He checked her work in the mirror and commented an emphatic, "Bueno."

He took her hand, and drew her next to him so they stood side by side, looking back at themselves in the glass.

"We make an attractive couple," he declared, as much to himself as to Iris. "Bueno," he repeated, satisfied. "Let us go."

* * *

Their short drive through the city concluded at the base of a series of grand steps, leading to a vast classical-style museum, the evening's imposing venue. Iris watched as gorgeous couple after gorgeous couple exited their cars and oh-so-stylishly began the long walk up to the entrance, their every move being captured by the many photographers lying in wait.

Iris fiddled with her dress self-consciously, feeling completely out of her depth. Sensing her discomfort, Sergio took her hands in his to steady them.

"You look beautiful," he said.

But before she could form a reply, Sergio's door was opened, and he had to step out. She had a moment to compose herself, then her own door was opened, accompanied by bursts of camera flashes. With Sergio there to receive her, she managed to leave the car somewhat gracefully, if with a little of the air of a rabbit caught in headlights. Standing there in the open, she felt panic rising until Sergio's hand took hers once more, and she was immediately reassured. He whispered into her ear, "Stay with me." Catching the worried expression on her face, he lifted her chin up gently, adding affectionately, "And try to smile, bella."

She held onto Sergio's hand tightly as he expertly led them past the photographers and along the seemingly endless walk to the safety of the museum.

The foyer of the building really was impressive, with its vast spaces and sumptuous marble, bringing to mind a Piranesi etching. The beautiful sounds of a string quartet playing Haydn floated in the background. Iris looked around her in wonder, trying to take it all in. Sergio steered her towards the hall where the other guests were congregating, and was immediately swamped by people wanting his attention.

Waiters milled around with glasses of champagne and delicious looking canapés. Sergio passed her a drink, but she turned down the appetisers — she just knew if she attempted to eat one, she'd either end up with the topping all over her dress, or someone would try to talk to her when she had her mouth full.

Her date was a man very much in demand; it seemed there was always someone waiting to talk to him. He introduced her to everyone he spoke to, and used English wherever possible. His hand rarely strayed far from her back, as if he knew she needed a bit of extra support in this unusual situation.

As Sergio schmoozed, Iris took the opportunity to appreciate her amazing surroundings — absolutely everything about the huge space seemed perfect: cream and gold featured strongly, with enormous chandeliers and lavish deep-red curtains adding the finishing touches to the opulence of the setting. Enormous windows looked out over large gardens illuminated by lanterns positioned along the winding walkways. She hoped they'd have a chance to explore them later.

When it was time to make their way into the dining room, Iris consulted the seating plan and, with dismay, found she wasn't going to be sitting next to Sergio, or even at the same table. Seeing her concerned expression, he explained that "couples" were never sat together at these events, but he'd ensured she had several English speakers at her table.

She needn't have worried: her table was very friendly, if more than slightly curious about how she came to be with Sergio. They tried to make their questioning subtle, but were quite clearly digging for details about their relationship. She gave nothing away, not knowing what, if anything, Sergio had said to any of these people about her and Paola. Some were potential business associates, and she really wasn't sure how much he would want her to share about their home situation. When her dining companions came to realise that she wasn't about to spill any dirty secrets about "Barcelona's most eligible bachelor" as one woman put it, the conversation relaxed and moved on to more neutral topics. Each of the ten courses was more delicious than the next, playfully presented and exquisite in every flavour, and soon the dialogue flowed almost as readily as the wine. Though she was a little unsure of how to tackle some of the more unusual dishes, she muddled through OK by copying what everyone else was doing. Despite their varying degrees of fluency in her language, everyone was very considerate, only occasionally breaking into Spanish to determine among themselves the correct English for something they were struggling to say; she felt very included.

Having relied so much on Sergio for the earlier part of the evening, Iris was glad to be standing on her own two feet more, yet intensely missed his company. She found the whole thing very confusing: being so carefully looked after by him was lovely, but deep down she still felt uneasy when she lowered her guard. It would be all too easy to let herself get carried away with the situation, particularly given how ambiguous their relationship was becoming. Nonetheless, it was reassuring when Sergio came over to check she was alright.

He was full of gossip and keen to point out anything he thought she might find amusing. He had a very good sense of humour. Though he made the most of being there, he was happy to laugh at himself and quick to spot any silliness and pomposity in the occasion. This was the Sergio she had fallen in love with, and she could feel her heart trying to pull them back together, however dangerous that would be. She pushed her glass of wine away: she needed to keep her head, even if she seemed to have no control over her heart.

But cool thinking could not control desire — once he'd returned to his own table, she couldn't help her gaze drifting over and they caught each other's eyes often, which she found both comforting and disconcerting.

When dinner was over, everyone began to slowly mill out of the dining room. Sergio appeared by Iris as she got up, she linked her arm through his, and they followed the others through to an enormous, ornate ballroom. A small string orchestra played Strauss, and some couples were already waltzing.

"Shall we?" Sergio asked, gesturing towards the dance floor.

Taking a gulp of champagne for courage, she nodded in agreement, and let guide her into the swirling throng.

She wasn't a fantastic dancer — had hardly twirled since her childhood lessons in fact — but she was having a lovely evening, and wanted to experience everything it had to offer. She marshalled her knowledge of the correct posture and steps. Self-conscious and hesitant, but determined to enjoy and make the most of it, she stood uncertainly in front of Sergio, and was relieved when he took her firmly in his arms, pulling her towards his strong, hard body, skilfully taking the lead. His movements were exact and confident. Under his expert guidance, she felt she was floating across the floor. She closed her eyes and allowed herself to become completely lost in the moment.

When the music eventually stopped, she sighed happily, relishing the last vestiges of the magic. She opened her eyes and was instantly met by Sergio's dark, hungry, intense gaze. Her heart pounded furiously. Her mind willed her to pull away, yet her body simply wouldn't let her. She tried to speak, but her throat was dry. He leant in even closer, his arousing masculine scent enveloping her. He whispered in her ear, "Are you ready to leave now, preciosa?" His tone and the proximity of his body to hers, left Iris in no doubt as to his intentions. She was once again powerless to resist him.

* * *

Sunlight filtered through the curtains, warming Iris's face and waking her from a deep, restful slumber. Stretching luxuriously, she suddenly registered the unfamiliar surroundings. She took in the large, sumptuous room and the crisp Egyptian-cotton sheets against her naked body. Smiling, she recalled the previous night, and glancing over to the other side of the king-size bed, felt a pang of disappointment at the empty depression making the absence of Sergio: knowing him, he'd got up early to check on something for work.

Iris savoured her sensual memories of the evening. Since that first night years ago, her mind had managed to block out the imprint of Sergio's touch, but her body certainly hadn't — each kiss had awakened long-buried responses. She blushed and shivered with pleasure as she recalled their lovemaking.

Getting up to find her lover, she saw her dress lying neatly over the back of a chair: she laughed at herself — however caught up in the moment she'd been, she'd made sure the dress was safe! Who knew if she'd ever have the chance to wear it again, but she certainly hoped so.

She picked up Sergio's crumpled shirt from the floor to provide some modesty; no matter how beautiful the ballgown was, it wasn't breakfast attire. Doing up the buttons, she inhaled deeply, taking in his heady scent.

As she went along the corridor towards the landing, she stopped when she heard voices downstairs. She could make out that one was Sergio's. The other was clearly female — and not Consuela. A tiny glimmer of mistrust intruded upon her good spirits. Just how long had Sergio been out of bed for? And who was he talking to? They certainly seemed to be enjoying each other's company, at least judging by the quickly hushed laughter wafting up to her.

Debating what to do, Iris heard Sergio and his mystery woman come out of the kitchen. Realising they'd spot her if they looked up, Iris darted away from the top of the stairs, positioning herself so she could just peep out from around a wall. Though not a perfect view, she couldn't quite see the front door, it was better than not knowing what was going on at all. Besides, it wasn't really spying; she was hardly properly dressed for introductions, anyway.

Sergio was whispering quietly in Spanish to his mystery visitor. Hmm, he obviously doesn't want me to discover what he's up to, Iris thought. She couldn't make out the woman's face, just the back of her head as she leant in to kiss Sergio before she left. Cheek or lips, she wondered with a hollow heart. Knowing Sergio's reputation, Iris had few doubts as to which.

As he shut the front door, she took the opportunity to flee and slip into her own bedroom. She was already undressed and in the shower when Sergio knocked.

"Can I come in?" he called out.

"I'm in the shower!" she replied.

"Maybe I could join you?" he suggested cheekily.

But Iris, hurt and confused, was in no mood for intimacy. "No, I'll be out in a few minutes," she called back. "I just need to pack and then we can go."

"Okay," he said, sounding perplexed.

Iris heard him leave and breathed a small sigh of relief: she really didn't want him to see her naked right now; she felt far too vulnerable. She'd be much more up to facing him when she was clothed and had her makeup on.

She scrubbed furiously at herself, going over and over again what she'd seen — would she never learn when it came to Sergio? They seemed to be doing pretty well with their co-parenting, so why did she have to give in to him again and mess everything up? He'd more than proved himself to be an excellent father, but he always treated her pretty appallingly. And she let him, time after time.

Paola should be her number-one priority, and she was. Iris knew that a stable home was extremely important for her daughter, and yet she'd gone and rocked the boat. It was imperative that her and Sergio's role as Paola's parents be calm and steady: Paola would pick up on animosity between them more and more as she got older, and that was the last thing Iris wanted.

She got herself ready and packed her bag. She left the ballgown in Sergio's room, but made sure it was back in its covering before she placed it carefully on his bed. She didn't know whether it was hers to keep, and would feel embarrassed asking.

Once she was certain she'd got all her belongings, and her head, together, she went downstairs, placing her bag by the front door. Making her way into the kitchen, she saw Sergio sitting at the table drinking coffee and studying some papers. He looked up with a smile as she came into the room, and immediately put his work to one side. He went to stand, but sensing the hostility radiating from Iris, sat straight down again.

"How are you, preciosa?" he asked, smiling but slightly tentative.

Images of the previous night flashed through her mind, and despite the gloom she'd worked herself up into, it took an awful lot of willpower for her not to smile back at him.

"I'm fine," she answered.

"Would you like a coffee?" he asked carefully.

"No, thank you," came the stiff reply.

"Is something wrong?" he asked with a small sigh.

"Nothing at all," she said, awaiting the right moment.

Silence fell as Sergio sipped his coffee. She slightly regretted turning down his offer of a drink, but that would have kept them there longer. She just wanted to get away from him, and back to Paola. Then she wouldn't have to deal with how hurt she was that he'd yet again gone straight from a bed he'd shared with her, into the arms of another woman. The adage, "a leopard never changes his spots," had never seemed more pertinent. She just wished she'd heeded it.

"Are we leaving soon?" she asked, eventually, when Sergio showed no sign of hurrying with his breakfast.

"We can call Miguel, if you like," he replied, sounding puzzled.

Taking her opening, she said: "Well, as long as you're sure you're finished with your girlfriend." But she could have kicked herself once the words were out of her mouth: she knew she sounded jealous and babyish, and totally unlike the sophisticated women Sergio must be used to.

"Ah," he said, as it became apparent to him what the problem was. "This is why you are . . ." he made a gesture, indicating her very negative body language. "My secretary, Carmen, came to drop off some very important contracts."

"It's really none of my business," she said stiffly.

"For some reason you thought I had a girlfriend here, I was merely correcting your mistaken assumption."

"Well, you two certainly sounded very secretive."

"You listened in on my conversation?"

"I couldn't," she admitted. "You were speaking Catalan and you weren't talking loudly enough."

"What were you doing trying to listen in to my work conversation?"

"I couldn't help it! I was coming downstairs to find out where you were." Her voice faltered, "I woke up and you'd gone." She ran a hand through her hair, "Is she the woman you went to the dinner with? That one I wouldn't come to with you?"

Sergio went from irritated to faintly amused, a smile playing at the corner of his lips.

"Yes, Carmen attended that function. And you saw her clearly you say?" he asked gently, trying his best not to laugh.

"Well, no, I was hiding at the top of the stairs, I didn't have a good view," she answered, trying to muster up as much dignity as she could.

"You really don't need to worry about Carmen."

"Oh, really?" she said, striving to appear blasé, and failing miserably.

"Carmen's lovely, she's great company. But she's also been married for more than thirty years and has three grown-up children."

"Oh."

"So you thought she and I . . .?"

"Yes," Iris replied, feeling extremely shamefaced.

"But I'd just been in bed with you," said an indignant Sergio.

"That's why I've been acting like a crazy woman."

"Why didn't you just ask me straight away?"

"I didn't think I needed to. I was so sure."

"Well, you were wrong. I never cheated on you. I would never cheat on you."

If he hadn't added that last sentence, she'd have started apologising profusely. Yet regardless of what had just happened in Sergio's hallway, three years ago he had cheated on her, and the pain from that betrayal still ran very deep. On a wave of emotion from all that bottled-up hurt, she blurted out, "What about before, when we first slept together?"

"I would never cheat on you," he repeated very seriously. "How could you think this of me?"

Without even registering his genuine upset, she shouted, "I know what happened!"

"The same as you know that I'm having an affair with my secretary?"

"What I know is that three years ago you went off with another woman, practically as soon as I was out of your bed!"

"And just who told you that?" he asked, but with that now-so-familiar glint in his dark eyes, which she knew meant he was close to losing his temper.

"You didn't show up to the office after I left you that morning, and then I overheard two of the secretaries talking — they said you'd cancelled everything and flown off somewhere exotic with your latest girlfriend — that obviously wasn't me as I was innocently at work!" she said, blinking hard in a desperate attempt to rein in the tears that threatened to fall as she remembered that horrible day.

Sergio's expression softened as he took in what she'd said and saw how distressed she'd become.

"I did book some time off," he said softly. "But not to go away with a woman. My father died. My mother called to tell me that he'd had a heart attack, just after you'd gone. I flew out to be with her immediately."

Iris began to get a horrible, horrible sinking feeling. She'd been so sure of his guilt and had never questioned her conclusion. Had she really got the situation so terribly wrong? Had she really been so incredibly stupid?

"I didn't have a phone number for you, but I emailed you that night at your work address to let you know where I was, and what was going on. I wanted you to come out to Spain and join me. You never replied."

He looked at her steadily, adding quietly, "I needed you."

She instinctively knew he was telling the truth. She felt awful, she'd let him down dreadfully. Why had she acted so hastily? If only she'd hung on at work another day, she'd have read his email. Maybe things between them could have been very different.

Iris was silent; she just couldn't think what to say. She had so much to apologise for, he'd missed out on the first two years of his daughter's life because of her. Where to begin?

He turned away and took his coffee cup over to the sink to rinse it, "Iris, there's got to come a point when you're going to have to trust me. I have no idea when that will be, but I really hope it's soon, because I'm getting tired of you always thinking I'm a villain."

He didn't give her a chance to speak and continued sadly, "I'm going to pack. I'll be ready to leave in fifteen minutes. Could you call Miguel to let him know, please? The number is by the phone."

As Iris watched him walk out of the room, she felt sick: she was losing him all over again, and it was completely her own fault.

Chapter 8

The ride back to Maria's house was conducted in silence. Even Miguel seemed to realise that something was wrong and refrained from his usual half-Catalan, half-English friendly chatter.

Iris tried a couple of times to meet Sergio's eyes, but she didn't know what she'd say even if she could get him to engage with her. The return journey certainly seemed to take a lot longer than the drive out to Barcelona the morning before. It was all she could do not to fling open the door and run into the house the second Miguel pulled up in front of the villa.

As always, her daughter cheered her up, though, and Iris found Paola with Maria, playing in the courtyard with a plastic tea set. She was very busy serving her much-loved àvia, but was thrilled to see her mother and father back, and allowed them to make a fuss of her for a while, then toddled back to her game.

Iris went straight upstairs to her room, giving the excuse that she wanted to get unpacked. Her head was in turmoil — how was she going to fix this? She'd let Sergio down and needed to show him how sorry she was for it all. Then she had to try to somehow regain his respect. Things had been so close to perfect between them, only yesterday. She didn't want to lose that, but had she already? Maybe they were just two people who weren't meant to be together, however much she wished that they could be.

Rehearsing how best to speak to him, she struggled to find the right words, or even where to start. Turning around with an armful of clothes, she jumped as she found the man himself standing in the doorway. Just how long he'd been there watching her, she wasn't sure. Iris felt she had to seize the opportunity now: the longer she left it, the worse her actions would seem, and the more hurt she would cause. Without a plan, she decided to dive right in, starting with the first of her blunders:

"Sergio," she said hurriedly, "I'm really sorry for what happened this morning, it was all my fault. Last night was amazing, and I don't want it to be spoilt by what came after."

He looked at her closely, as though working out whether she was being genuine. He doubts me as much as I doubt him, she thought to herself sadly.

"Nothing could spoil last night for me, preciosa," he finally said, coming over and tenderly wrapping her in his strong, tanned arms. "I am sorry, too. Nothing should have taken me away from you this morning. If I hadn't organised for Carmen to drop the documents round yesterday, I would be where I belong — in bed with you."

She felt her knees go weak as he spoke the words she'd been yearning to hear. Yet she couldn't let herself get sidetracked — it wouldn't be right to give in to his caresses now, she still had to apologise for the biggest mistake of her life.

He looked surprised when she gently disentangled herself from his embrace.

Taking his hands in hers, she began, "I was completely wrong not to tell you about my pregnancy, and I'm so, so sorry for it. I believed I was doing the right thing, for Paola as well as for myself. But I didn't think of you, and that wasn't fair. I stole your daughter's first years from you, and I wish I could turn the clock back. You're such a wonderful father. I'm so sorry." By now her voice was shaking and, despite all her attempts to remain composed, tears filled her eyes. She looked up at him pleadingly and asked, "Is there any way you can learn to forgive me?"

He returned her pleading gaze with one of tenderness, "Iris, I forgave you long ago." He gave her hand a reassuring squeeze. "You adore Paola, and I know you'd have only made the decisions you thought were in her best interests. You were wrong, but I understand what you did. I'm not completely blameless myself — if my pride hadn't stopped me, I could have found you as soon as I got back from my father's funeral and put things right between us. I would have found out about Paola and been there for you both." Taking Iris in his arms once more, he whispered softly, "It's all in the past. It's the future we need to think of now."

"But why do we keep messing things up?" she asked, the question playing on her mind.

"That I don't know," he said. "I think sometimes we are both very unsure of each other perhaps. This will change in time." He kissed her gently on the forehead, "Come. My mother's waiting outside, she has something she wants to talk to us about."

* * *

Iris had to be patient when they'd got down to the courtyard. An excited Maria spoke rapidly in Catalan to Sergio, gesticulating wildly in her enthusiasm.

With a stern prod, Maria then signalled for Sergio to translate to Iris.

"My mother thinks we should have a party tomorrow night."

"A party?" Iris said.

"Yes, a proper party for the whole family." Sergio reached over to touch his mother's hand when he said this.

Despite Maria's clear excitement, Iris could see the trace of sorrow on her face. "It will be the first party since my father died," Sergio added, "She says she finally has something to celebrate with us and Paola being here."

"What a lovely idea," Iris said warmly, and embraced Maria. "Would you ask your mother if there's anything I can do to help?"

Sergio duly passed on the message, and translated the reply: "No, just relax, be happy, and make sure you look your most beautiful for my son."

Iris felt the heat of a bright red blush on her cheeks immediately. She was so unsure of what was going on between her and Sergio that it seemed bizarre for people to comment on them as if they were a properly established couple. She wasn't sure what to say. After all that had gone on between them upstairs, she was hopeful they might finally be starting to get things right, but they, and just they, still had much to work out.

Thankfully, Iris was saved further awkwardness by Paola, who came bouncing over, diverting everyone's attention, allowing Iris's face to return to its usual colour.

Maria went shopping after lunch with her eldest daughter, Isabel, so Iris, Sergio and Paola had the house to themselves. While Paola had her nap, Iris took the opportunity to finish unpacking. Her bedroom was nice and cool, and she was pleased to have a moment to think — truth be told, as much as she wanted to sort matters out between her and Sergio, she was also apprehensive. What exactly was going to happen between them? In the long run, what would be best for them all?

If she went with her instincts, then Iris knew she craved Sergio: she'd never felt as powerful an attraction to any other man. She'd known that all along, but spending such an amazing night with him had made this absolutely clear. Yet it wasn't as simple as going on a couple of dates and seeing what developed — they had a daughter together. If they did get involved again, and things fell apart, it might hurt Paola terribly.

And what about herself? Did she love him? Or rather, did she still love him? It had taken her a very long time to get over Sergio, if she ever really had. The thought of letting down her defences again terrified her: if their relationship failed, was she strong enough to survive losing him again?

There was also Sergio's work to consider — he was married to his business, did he have room in his life for her? But then how much of this opinion was based on the man she used to know? Yes, Sergio worked hard, but now he made time for Paola, and seemed able to switch off from his job. He'd been affected by his father's death, it had shifted his outlook. Work no longer ran his life.

Iris heard Paola wake up and went to get her from next door. Coming out of her room, she bumped into Sergio, who grabbed her arms to steady her, his manly scent disturbing her equilibrium far more than their collision.

"I was coming to see if you wanted a drink," he explained, brushing some stray hairs back from her face.

"Oh, yes please," she replied, her worries momentarily forgotten.

"Okay, you get Paola and I'll meet you in the courtyard with some sangria."

He kissed her casually on the mouth, leaving a breathless Iris with shivers down her spine and a big smile on her face. There and then, she made the decision: any man who made her feel that good, was worth the risk of getting hurt for.

* * *

Outside, Iris and Paola found Sergio preparing a tub of water for Paola to play with. The little girl was soon happily soaking wet and pouring water from her plastic teapot all over the flagstones. The garden walls cast plenty of shade, so even though the day was still hot, it was comfortable to sit out in the late-summer air, sipping their refreshing drinks.

Iris moved herself into the sun, tilting her head back and enjoying the warmth on her face. She'd been a fool to have ever been reluctant to come to Spain. It made her quite sad to think what awaited Paola when they eventually went back to London: to go from this heavenly place, surrounded by a family who adored her, to their tiny flat. To swap this beautiful, rugged landscape, for the confines of London. She didn't let herself dwell on it for long: Sergio hadn't mentioned when they would be heading back, and, for the moment at least, Iris certainly wasn't going to ask.

Relaxed, she closed her eyes, enjoying the happy, contented sounds of Sergio and Paola playing together. She must have dozed off because when she opened her eyes, the sun had moved position and Paola's excited squeals now came from round the other side of the house. Oh, the luxury of having someone to help look after her daughter, so she could just fall asleep in the sun every now and again and not be on constant toddler-watching duty. This would be what life could always be like, she thought, if she and Sergio were together. They would be a proper family.

* * *

As the shadows drew in, the evening's birdsong started in earnest. Maria had returned, and they'd enjoyed a light supper together out in the aromatic evening air, before an exhausted Paola was carried up to bed.

"Iris, I have something I wish to speak to you about," Sergio announced once the supper things had been cleared away. "Will you walk with me?"

Maria gave them an encouraging smile as Sergio took Iris's hand and led her into the garden. His mother certainly wasn't subtle about her hopes that they'd become a couple.

He took her to a part of the garden she hadn't seen, a sort of hidden enclave, where an old stone bench could just about be distinguished from the plants surrounding it. They sat down on it.

"My father proposed to my mother on this seat almost forty-five years ago," he began, stroking the lichen-covered slab absentmindedly as he spoke. She waited for him to continue, not sure why he'd brought her here to tell her this, and wondering where it was leading.

"I've been focussed on business for many years, but there are more important things, I think."

He took a moment, composing exactly what he wanted to say.

"I'd been debating what to do since my father died. How I could have a better balance in my life. And then I discovered Paola. She was the push I needed."

Iris went to respond, but he held up his hand to stop her, "Please, allow me to finish," he said. "I have been working towards moving my affairs back to Spain, to be closer to my family. And obviously Paola is now a very important part of that family. I brought you both here hoping you'd fall in love with Spain, and realise what a wonderful country it is to raise a child in."

Iris was confused and disappointed. She hadn't been sure what to expect, but this wasn't what she'd hoped for.

"So you tricked me," she stated. "This wasn't just a business trip. Could you have flown back to England before, when I wanted to?"

"I did have plenty of work to do here, but only because of relocating the business," he admitted.

Realising how badly this was coming across, he swiftly went on, "I wanted you and Paola to experience life in Spain. The longer we were here, the more like a family we felt. I thought that would end if we went back to the UK, and I didn't want it to."

"But we're not really a family, Sergio. Paola and I are only here because you led me to believe I had no other option than to stay," she interrupted angrily.

A flash of hurt crossed Sergio's face, and she felt guilty — what she'd said had come out harsher than she'd meant it to.

"I really thought that if you gave life here a chance, you'd want to stay, that's why I encouraged you to wait before making a decision about the promotion you were offered. But if you choose to return to London now, I understand," he said. "I will not try to stop you. Of course I won't force you to stay anywhere you're not happy."

"What about you and Paola?"

"I must be a real father to her, like my own father was to me. I'll abandon my plans, and move back to the UK if you decide to live there permanently. I just ask that you allow Paola to visit my family sometimes. They are all very much in love with her."

"Of course they'll get to see Paola wherever we live," she said tenderly.

He drew a deep breath, as though to brace himself.

Oh dear, what's coming now? Iris thought.

"There is one more thing I wanted to speak to you about." He paused yet again, "Tradition is very important to my family, and to me. My mother and father were married for many years, all my sisters are married. We have a daughter together, and it isn't right that her parents are separate. I think last night proves that we are attracted to each other."

She blushed as the memories came flooding back to her. There was certainly no denying there could be passion between the two of them, but surely he wasn't about to do what she suspected? With mounting horror, she watched as he went down on one knee and took her hand in his.

"Iris, would you do me the honour of becoming my wife?" he asked huskily.

He'd really done it hadn't he? How on earth was she supposed to respond? How could he possibly think this was a good idea?

As parents, she and Sergio could complement each other well, and goodness, was she attracted to him! But what was Sergio thinking talking about marriage now? She wanted a relationship with him, and of course she'd fantasised about them being a more traditional family. But at present, they could barely manage a day without an argument. Did he love her? He'd never said so. Did she love him . . .? Did she? Yes, she finally admitted — she'd never really stopped. Her feelings may have been hidden away, yet they were definitely still there.

Finding her voice, she answered, "Sergio, it's really lovely of you to bring me here, and propose where your father did, but we're not even dating properly. What makes you think we're ready to get married?"

"We have a daughter . . ."

"Yes, I am aware of that, but it doesn't mean we have to get married! We spend most of our time together fighting!"

"But the making up has been such good fun," he said, trying to lighten the mood with a naughty grin.

Endeavouring to ignore how sexy he looked, she muttered an evasive, "I need some time to think," as firmly as she could manage.

"Of course. How long?" he replied.

She smiled at his impatience. Marriage was a huge step: she did love Sergio, of that she was now certain, and she did truly want to be with him, but did his feelings run as deep for her? Why was he doing this? Did he really want her for herself, or did he just want Paola's mother? She was sure he was attracted to her, but was that enough to base a lifetime of commitment to each other on?

"I don't know," she answered truthfully, "Let me think it over." She kissed him on his cheek, and got up to leave. He gently stopped her with a hand on her arm, "Iris," he said, "I am very sorry to have misled you about staying in Spain. I swear to you, my intentions were good, even if I went about my plans the wrong way. Please consider my proposal carefully, imagine how Paola would love it, us all joined as a real family."

She nodded, too unsure of herself and all the contradictory feelings swimming about inside her to do anything more, and went back to the house.

Entering the kitchen, she was warmly greeted by Maria and offered coffee, and yet more food. She accepted the coffee, but didn't stay to chat for long. Instead, she slipped out into the courtyard, hoping to find somewhere quiet to collect her thoughts. As she gazed across the twilight shaded garden, her eyes fell on Sergio's treehouse.

She checked to ensure no one was watching her, although she didn't quite know why she was being so secretive. Maybe because she saw the treehouse Sergio's private place, she felt guilty using it.

She climbed the rickety ladder and entered the wooden sanctuary. There she sat, sipping her hot drink, trying to get her head round all that Sergio had said. Well, first of all, he'd lied to her. He'd made her come with him and kept her here, even though in the beginning she'd been unhappy about this. He'd led her to believe that if she left with Paola, he'd take custody of their daughter. These actions were pretty inexcusable, but strangely she found herself forgiving him. He'd treated both her and Paola extremely well: he'd been kind, generous, and supportive. His big, busy family had been wonderful for Paola, and for her as well. And he'd only done it because he felt it was the right thing for everyone, he wanted his whole family to be together. Isn't that what would be best for Paola?

But what about his marriage proposal? She really hadn't been expecting that, yet he wasn't just asking on a whim, it was a sincere and considered request. The Sergio she knew, rarely did anything on impulse, he was a planner. He was completely serious.

It was past midnight when Iris climbed down from the treehouse and wearily made her way back to the villa. The kitchen light had been left on for her, but there was no sign that anybody else was up.

Going upstairs, she saw Sergio's door was shut. She hesitated outside it, unsure whether to knock and see if he was awake. She desperately wanted to. Her whole body ached to feel him against her again. But she knew if she went to him now she was likely to get caught up in the heat of the moment and accept his proposal though her mind was still in turmoil.

Using every ounce of will-power she possessed, she crept past, quickly checked on Paola, and went into her own bedroom. She hoped a good night's sleep might make everything clearer for her.

* * *

Iris most definitely did not come from the sort of family who threw impromptu parties, especially not on the scale Maria was planning. Sergio's sisters had begun cooking at the crack of dawn, or so it seemed to Iris when she poked her head into the kitchen to make some coffee and breakfast at eight. Everything was already in full swing, saucepans bubbling away on every available part of the stove, and surfaces covered in flour and mixing bowls. Iris felt embarrassed to be only just out of bed and in her pyjamas, but no one seemed to mind. She was handed a coffee from the big pot that had just been made, and toast was produced for her and Paola before she'd even asked if there was room for her to make some.

Paola joined her cousins in the sitting room, where they were watching cartoons and munching their breakfasts. Iris took her coffee back upstairs where she had a quick shower and got dressed.

When she returned, the children had finished their breakfast and were helping out in the kitchen. Although too young to be much help, Paola seemed determined to do her bit and was thrilled to have her own tea towel to dry her pink plastic cup.

* * *

The preparations carried on all day. Iris did her best to assist wherever possible, even if it was just keeping the children entertained and out from under everybody's feet. Long trestle tables seemed to appear from nowhere and were set up in the garden, covered in cheerful checked cloths.

Carlos, one of Sergio's brothers-in-law, arrived with a car full of wine. An old tin bath was excavated from the depths of an outbuilding, dusted off, and filled with ice to chill the drinks as Maria's fridge was already stuffed to bursting point with all the food.

Candles were placed on the tables and small wrought-iron lanterns set up along the garden paths and around the outside of the house ready for when darkness fell.

Iris hardly saw Sergio, who was kept busy by his mother and sisters. He was in constant motion: lifting, carrying, and picking things up from the houses of various family members. He seemed so different from his suited work self — in his office he was in complete control, and yet here he appeared quite happy to be bossed around by numerous diminutive women.

* * *

At five all work ceased, and everyone either returned to their homes or went up to their rooms to get ready. A sense of anticipation hung heavy in the air. Even Paola picked up on the excitement and insisted upon wearing the princess dress Sergio had bought her, complete with its crown. She watched Iris putting on her make-up and helped to brush her hair.

At six, Iris began to hear cars pull up and people arriving. The sound of excited chatter drifted in through the window. She took Paola's hand and helped her down the stairs to greet everybody. Iris was nervous, knowing she would be meeting plenty of Sergio's extended family, relatives she'd never met before. They'd all be wondering about her and Sergio's relationship, just as she was herself. She was not much closer to having a proper answer for Sergio. She loved him, and wanted nothing more than for the two of them to be together and form a real family with Paola, and possibly more children in the future. But it all seemed too soon, too rushed. Was she being overly cautious though? Should she just take a risk and grab the opportunity to become Sergio's wife? She really didn't know. She was aware that part of the reason she was undecided was that she wondered why Sergio was so anxious to take such an enormous leap forward in their relationship — it had come completely out of the blue. Had his sisters and mother talked him into it by making him feel guilty about having a child out of wedlock? She hoped this wasn't the case, but he did come from a very traditional family. She certainly didn't want to accept his proposal if it was only because his mother had told him to do it!

Well, there was no time to worry about it anymore now; she had a very excited little girl, desperate to join in the fun. Putting her concerns aside, she and Paola made their entrance into the party.

Chatting and mingling, it wasn't long before Iris was able to relax and was thoroughly enjoying herself. In fact, it would have been very hard not to as Sergio's family were all being so friendly and were clearly anxious to ensure she didn't feel like an outsider and was welcomed as one of them. She kept one eye on Paola, who was happily running around with her cousins as usual, chattering away in a mixture of English and the Catalan she'd picked up over the past weeks.

The feast was served at eight, and everything Iris tasted was absolutely delicious. How so much had been prepared in just a matter of hours was a mystery. Paella, tortilla, salads, fish, salamis and jamon, breads — platters and platters full of food covered the tables so it was almost possible to imagine them groaning under the enormous weight.

* * *

Paola fell asleep in her mother's arms around ten, and Iris gently carried her up to her room and popped her into bed.

Rejoining the party in the garden, she was met by Sergio, who handed her a drink. It had been so long since he'd been back to Spain for anything other than a flying visit, that he'd had many relations desperate to catch up. This was the first chance he and Iris had had to be together that evening, despite many darting glances between them.

"This party is just wonderful," she said, taking a sip of the delicious chilled white wine.

"Yes, it's good to have the whole family together, it doesn't happen often."

"Maria looks very happy."

"Yes, family is what she loves."

There was silence as they each drank and took in the scene.

"Thank you for bringing Paola here. To meet my mother and sisters, I mean," Sergio said.

"I'm glad I did."

"You've made it very easy for them," said Sergio, "But my mother is very . . . old-fashioned. She does not understand why we are not married."

"Oh."

"For her a child needs their mother and father to be together," he explained.

"Well sometimes things don't work out quite the way we'd like," Iris said. "Life isn't always straightforward."

"My mother has been putting pressure on me."

"Pressure?" She stared fixedly down the avenue of lanterns, gathering her thoughts.

"Yes."

"So is that why you wanted to marry me?" she asked.

"When we are married, everyone will be happy," he said, evading the question.

"Is that why you wanted to marry me?"

He opened his mouth as if to reply, but kept silent, seeming to change his mind about what best to say.

Well, I guess that answers my question, Iris thought sadly. And I suppose I know my answer to his question now too. She felt deflated and just wanted to go inside and curl up in bed.

Turning so she was looking him straight in the face, she hesitantly started to speak, "Sergio, I'm sorry. . .", but got no further as the hubbub was unexpectedly hushed by the sound of a fork tapping against a champagne glass. Maria was standing in the courtyard, glass in hand, ready to make a toast. The whole party gathered around her to listen.

Unable to follow the rapid Catalan, Iris looked to Sergio for help and found he was no longer by her side. He had moved to join Maria at the centre of the crowd. Putting his arm around his mother, he took over her speech.

Iris was tired and confused, and unable to understand most of what was being said, so let her gaze wander skywards. Planning just what she was going to say to Sergio when he'd finished, she suddenly heard cheers and applause, and was engulfed by what seemed like every member of the party, hugging and kissing her. She smiled nervously back, wanting to appear friendly, but with no idea what was going on.

Ushered through the crowd, she ended up next to Sergio. He took her hand and kissed it, at which point the applause and cheering became deafening.

"What's going on?" Iris hissed, struggling to maintain her fixed grin.

"I've announced that we're getting married."

Momentarily stunned into silence, Iris was enveloped by a joyously tearful Maria, and then by the rest of Sergio's family. In amongst all the congratulatory hugging and kissing that ensued, the "engaged" couple were separated, and Iris's stuttered protestations went unheard. As the excitement started to die down, she discovered that Sergio had disappeared.

* * *

Having finally managed to make her excuses and leave, Iris rushed into the house and practically ran up the stairs, fired by the fury she felt towards Sergio for placing her in such an embarrassing situation. Why had he done it? She'd made it clear she needed time to make her decision. At no point had she said yes to him — there was no possibility of a misunderstanding. Perhaps it was his weird idea of a joke? But then surely he wouldn't involve his whole family, and he really hadn't looked like he was joking.

Iris burst into Sergio's bedroom, without pausing to knock. He wasn't there. Blast. Where was he? Chasing after him would do no good; they could end up going round in circles missing each other all night. And she didn't want to go back downstairs. She decided to wait. Sitting at the foot of the bed, she fumed over what had just happened, her angry thoughts at odds with the sounds drifting up from the party, continuing merrily outside. Did he really think she'd just marry him because he'd told all his relatives she'd said yes? She knew Sergio could be impatient, but she hadn't thought him capable of this just because she'd said she needed some time to think about his proposal! Just how was he going to explain to Maria when the "engagement" was called off? What a mess he'd made!

The minutes passed. She looked at the clock by the bedside: it was almost midnight. The festivities were still in full swing, goodness only knew when he'd make an appearance. Feeling a wave of tiredness wash over her, she knew she needed to go to bed. Resolving to deal with Sergio in the morning, she dejectedly wandered back to her own room.

* * *

When Iris came downstairs with Paola the following day, the clean-up was well underway. Sergio was absent, apparently he'd gone out on some errands for his mother. Frustrated, Iris grabbed a pair of rubber gloves, and got stuck into some washing-up, despite Maria's protests.

Eventually she spotted Sergio's car pulling into the driveway. At last! Stepping away from the sink, she counted to three to compose herself, resolving not to hit him over the head with a dirty frying pan, no matter how satisfying it would be. Glancing through a window on her way out of the kitchen, he was nowhere to be seen. For goodness' sake, where had he gone now? She peered intently through the glass, trying to spot him. Nothing: no sign anywhere. She gave a startled shriek and jumped when his face unexpectedly materialised at the window.

"Were you looking for me?" he asked breezily, without a care in the world, and as if he had no idea she might be livid and seriously considering reverting to the frying pan if she didn't get some answers from him soon.

"Yes, I was. I need to speak to you right now," Iris practically growled, making sure he was left in no doubt that she would not be put off.

"Okay," he replied calmly, "Shall we go into the courtyard? I think it's empty."

"Fine, I'll meet you there in a minute," she said. She hurried through the house and out the back door, not wanting to give him any chance to wander off or begin talking to anyone else. She needn't have worried. He was waiting as promised, sat in one of the wrought-iron chairs that surrounded a matching table. He had his face up to the sun, basking in its warmth, and seemed completely relaxed and at ease — the total opposite of how she felt.

"I assume you want to talk about our engagement," he pre-empted as she stomped up to begin her harangue.

"You could have the decency to look at least a bit embarrassed!"

"Come now, preciosa, you can't be cross with me for wanting to announce our big news when all my family were together, it was the perfect opportunity! You wanted time to get used to the idea, and I waited as long as I could."

"But I hadn't said yes!"

"You were going to."

"You assumed I'd say yes? Why?" she asked, stunned.

"You find me attractive, don't you? I can provide for you and care for you. But mainly I thought you'd want what was best for Paola," he said bluntly.

"Of course I want what's best for Paola," she replied, shocked he'd suggest anything to the contrary.

"So you don't agree that having her parents married would be better for her?"

"Not if her parents aren't happily married."

He stood and turned away from Iris. "We are getting married," he said with finality. "Paola deserves a stable family home, and I will give it to her."

Iris felt heartbroken. She'd hoped she and Sergio had got beyond this; hoped they'd grown closer while in Spain, and that he respected her. She was now certain that he didn't.

"I need to return to Barcelona to work for a few days. You and Paola can stay here — she's happy with her cousins around, and my family will be able to help you plan the wedding. This morning I spoke to the priest, he will marry us next Saturday."

He stole a glance at her. Seeing the horrified expression on her face, he paused and reached for her hand. She listlessly allowed him to take it, too dazed to do anything else.

"Next Saturday?" she repeated quietly, more to herself than to him.

"There's no point in waiting, and I'm assuming you don't want a big wedding."

"No, but . . ."

"You will see, preciosa, it is for the best. We will be a family."

Sergio's eyes looked sad, almost regretful, she realised.

"And where do you think we'll live?" she asked.

"In my apartment in Barcelona."

"What if I don't want to live there?" Iris enquired without anger: somehow at this point she was more curious than anything — just what was he thinking? What else had he arranged without her knowledge?

"Of course we can move if you'd prefer," he said gently. "We can live wherever you want."

"What if I want to live in my flat? My flat in London."

A flash of irritation crossed his face. He stared at her, as if trying to gauge whether she was merely being awkward. "I would rather we lived in Spain so that we can be close to my family. If you are really against this then we can discuss moving back to London, but we will keep a home in Spain and visit during Paola's school holidays. We could not fit comfortably in your flat, and the area is not safe, so no, we will not be living there."

When she didn't react, he continued, "Preciosa, just imagine how much better life will be for you. You'll have me to help with Paola, the money to do whatever you wish. You can give up your work if you'd like. Paola will have her parents together, and she'll have everything she needs, she'll never want for anything."

Woken from her daze by his last comment, Iris snapped: "As I've made quite clear, Sergio, our daughter has always had everything she needs. You make it sound like she spent the first couple of years of her life completely deprived!"

"I didn't mean it like that, Iris. You've done a wonderful job bringing up Paola, but you've got to admit that having people to help makes things a lot easier, and you must have struggled for money when you were on your own."

"I'm not going to talk about this anymore. It seems you've made up your mind about my life. I suppose you think I should be grateful you're letting me know we're getting married at all! Wouldn't it have been easier to have simply taken me to the church on the day with no warning?" She began walking back into the house. "I'm going to find Paola."

The little girl was just finishing a story with Maria, and Iris whisked her daughter upstairs to her room. She was resolved to leave; she couldn't possibly stay here now. Did Sergio honestly expect her to marry him like this? She loved him, she really did: it had been staring her in the face for so long, but she hadn't seen it, or hadn't wanted to see it. She wanted to be with him, but why couldn't he want her for herself? Why couldn't it just be simple? Why couldn't he just love her and allow her the time she needed, and not act like a spoilt, arrogant child?

She brought out some toys for Paola to play with and pulled their suitcases out from under the bed. Her feverish packing was quite cathartic: doing something about the situation, even if it was just leaving, gave her some feeling of control. Though how exactly she was going to get to an airport from the middle of nowhere was something she hadn't quite solved yet. Neither had she worked out how to get flight times without any internet — her Catalan was still rather lamentable, certainly not up to phone conversations with directory enquiries.

There'd be lots of flights available to London from Barcelona airport, so all she really needed was to get hold of a taxi to take her the two hour drive to the city. But she wondered how much that would cost.

She became aware that Paola was watching her intently. "Are you alright, sweetheart?" Iris asked.

"Where's Papa?"

"I'm not sure, probably helping Àvia with something."

"I help, too?" asked Paola hopefully.

"No, you can help me instead. You can get me your socks."

Paola dutifully fetched her socks from the chest of drawers in the adjoining room.

"What you doing, Mama?" the little girl inquired.

"I'm packing our things, darling. We're leaving. We're going home."

"To Consuela?"

"No sweetheart," Iris replied, hiding her hurt, "Not Papa's house in Barcelona. We're going back to our flat in London. To your old bedroom and your cot, and all your old toys."

Paola looked confused then asked, "Is Papa coming?"

"No, he's got work to do here, but we'll see him very soon."

"Is Àvia coming?"

"No darling, Àvia lives here."

Paola's face scrunched up as she began to cry.

"Oh, come here, sweetie," said Iris, sitting on the bed and lifting her daughter onto her knee. Paola cuddled into her mother. "Don't you want to go home and see all your things? What about your friends at playgroup? They'll all be missing you."

"I want Papa," the little girl sobbed.

Iris felt dreadful. Nothing was ever easy, was it? Could she really do this? No matter how angry she was, did she really have the right to tear Sergio and Paola apart again as casually as this? She'd already been responsible for father and daughter missing those wonderful first years because of her rash judgements. Was she close to making the same mistake again?

There was also the wonderful Maria to consider. She'd been so kind and welcoming, when she could have made things quite awkward. It would be heartless for Iris just to storm out taking Maria's beloved granddaughter with her.

Taking into account her own feelings, and trying to be totally honest with herself, Iris didn't actually want to leave Spain. There was so much more here for them than in London.

And despite his controlling arrogance, she loved Sergio and ached for him. During the calms between their storms, what they had was special. They'd been tentatively building "something" together before this bombshell. Could they get over this? In the end, what was it he wanted? To marry her. To always be with her. Exactly what she also desired, more than anything. If she put aside her pride for everyone's sake and went along with his plans, could he learn to love her as she did him? When she'd envisaged getting engaged, it wasn't anything like this, she thought sadly, but then life wasn't a fairy tale, it would never be perfect. If she accepted his offer, she'd be marrying the man she loved and doing the best for her daughter, surely that should be good enough for her?

His proposal couldn't purely have been down to some sense of obligation: she meant a lot to him, she was certain of that, and if his behaviour in bed was anything to go by, he found her as attractive as she found him. Surely you couldn't have a stronger foundation for love to grow?

Looking into her daughter's tear-filled eyes, there was only one decision she could make. Suppressing her doubts, her hurt and her worry, she kissed Paola gently on the forehead, "I'll never take you away from Papa, darling. We both love you so much. There's no need for tears. Mama's going to stop being silly. Come on, sweetheart, let's tidy this up and then we can go and play."

She might not be having her dream wedding, but she would marry Sergio for everyone's sake, and hope it would all turn out for the best in the end.

Paola helped her mother put her socks back in the drawer, her happiness restored. They went downstairs to join everyone for lunch, Iris fighting her heartache and hoping her daughter wouldn't mention how close they'd been to fleeing. She may have decided to stay and go along with Sergio's hasty wedding plans, but Iris was angry about the way she'd been treated and resolved to say as little as possible to him besides what was absolutely necessary.

Drawing him aside after the meal, she curtly informed him, "I'll marry you on Saturday. You're conceited and thoughtless, but you're right: Paola deserves us both."

Ignoring his pleased reply, she made it plain she didn't want him anywhere near her, and marched off.

She largely avoided Sergio for the remainder of the day and went to bed early: it should be quite clear that she had no interest in any ideas he might have about them acting like a real engaged couple.

* * *

Lingering in her room for longer than usual the following morning, Iris hoped to miss Sergio at the breakfast table, knowing he was leaving early for Barcelona. She succeeded, but found a note waiting for her outside her room. Paola was hungry, and eager to get downstairs for something to eat. Not wanting to look at it in front of Maria, Iris left the letter on the bed to read later.

Iris ate her breakfast and left Paola making cakes with her grandmother. She planned to get some work done, but wanted to read Sergio's letter first. Sitting down on the bed, she opened the envelope and discovered an extremely comprehensive list of what needed to be done for the wedding. As usual, he seemed to have thought of everything: there were contact details for florists, caterers, a band, a photographer etc., etc., meticulous and complete, nothing escaped his attention. Under "dress" he'd simply written, "Speak to my mother."

Well, she certainly wasn't going to go right back downstairs to discuss what she was going to wear on the "big day": she accepted she'd need to face up to the urgent preparations soon, but could just about avoid it all for a while longer, especially as she'd decided against inviting anyone from London – it would be awful enough to get through the wedding without her friends around asking questions and wondering why she wasn't more excited and why everything was so rushed. Besides, she really did have some proof-reading she needed to get done, ready to be emailed once she had an internet connection again.

Sergio telephoned that evening to speak to Paola. Suspecting it was him, Iris tried to make herself scarce, but it wasn't long before she heard Maria call out that he also wanted to talk to her. Maria appeared to have no idea that there was anything wrong between her son and his bride-to-be, and she handed the telephone over with a conspiratorial smile.

Iris waited until she'd left the room, then opened the conversation with a perfunctory, "Hello," and was impressed by how well she kept her temper when he immediately responded, "Have you begun the wedding preparations?"

"No, Sergio, I haven't," she said, "I've been looking after our daughter and working."

"Surely you could have at least made a start, there's a lot to do and not long to do it all in."

"Yes, I know. You very kindly informed me of when my wedding day would be. It's not something I'm likely to forget."

"Would you rather I had Carmen arrange it all?" he said after a short pause.

"If that's what you want, then fine. I'm sure she'll be able to organise everything exactly as you'd want it."

He sighed, "Okay, I will deal with it. But you must speak to my mother about the dress."

"I'll go and talk to her now," she replied resignedly.

"Then we'll meet on Thursday: we must go together to see Father Garcia who will marry us. I plan to go direct to the church and wait for you at midday. Miguel will drive you. Please do not be late."

"I wouldn't dream of it," she said and put down the phone.

She put Paola to bed and then searched for Maria. She found her future mother-in-law bent in the garden, deadheading roses.

Getting straight to the point, Iris began Sergio's request in her hesitant Catalan, then abruptly realised she didn't know the word for "wedding dress". It was a hard one to mime, and they both started giggling, making the gestures all the more difficult to follow, but eventually she did make herself understood. Thrilled, Maria led her inside the house up to the attic. Holding torches, they climbed up a ladder into the dark, musty-smelling space.

Their torches illuminated boxes piled everywhere. The place was crammed full: it didn't look like the family had ever thrown anything out. Maria edged her way to a chest hidden away in one of the corners. Disturbed dust drifted into the air, dancing in their torch beams as she rummaged. Eventually she triumphantly pulled out a carefully wrapped linen bundle and beckoned to Iris to follow her back down the ladder.

In her bedroom, Maria reverently unwound the covering, explaining in a mixture of English, Catalan, and gestures, that inside was her own wedding dress. All her daughters had taken after their father and were much larger than her petite frame; none of them had been able to wear the gown on their wedding day. Maria was offering it to Iris.

It was truly beautiful. Made of pale cream silk with intricate and incredibly delicate embroidery covering the bodice, it had a gorgeous portrait neckline, trumpet silhouette and basque waist. It was timelessly elegant, and was exactly the sort of dress Iris had always dreamed of getting married in, surrounded by a big, happy family, just like Sergio's. And yet it was all she could do to hold back her tears as she hugged Maria in thanks. Claiming she could hear Paola calling for her, she made a very swift exit from the room.

* * *

Iris met Sergio outside the church on Thursday as instructed. She acknowledged him with a nod and waited while he spoke to Miguel. "I'll drive you back," he explained as Miguel drove off. They walked in together.

The air inside was cool and her eyes took a while to adjust to the dim light of the interior. Each of her steps rang out as she walked down the stone aisle with Sergio. She tried hard not to imagine what it would be like when she walked down the same aisle in just a few days.

She felt swamped by the sheer vastness of the church. It was huge and echoey, and she was uncomfortable. She wasn't particularly religious, but it seemed wrong to be in this sacred place, planning to make promises in front of a priest as well as all Sergio's family when she felt as she did. Promises which she'd agree to in another language, but which, nonetheless, she understood. She knew she'd be swearing to love, honour, and obey Sergio. Well, the love part wasn't a problem for her, though it might weigh on Sergio's conscience, she thought to herself. But could she really promise to honour and obey him when he showed her so little respect, and she was hoping, rather than certain, it would work out? Somehow, saying the vows here in this setting was wrong unless they both loved each other like a man and wife should, and were sure about what they were committing to. She would much rather have got married quickly in a registry-office ceremony with just a couple of witnesses. Maybe that way she wouldn't feel such a hypocrite.

The priest greeted Sergio warmly and familiarly. Maria had told her that Father Garcia had christened Sergio and had affectionately scolded him throughout his boyhood for various minor transgressions. He was very old and small, with tanned, extremely wrinkled skin. He welcomed Iris with a kind smile.

The priest talked them through what would happen during the service. Sergio translated everything, but in her resentment, Iris pointedly didn't thank him. She would have preferred that this part of the wedding planning could also have been done without her.

Once the priest had finished going over the essentials, Iris took herself off to have a proper look around the church while Sergio and Father Garcia continued arranging matters. She wandered through the shadows, over to a stand of votive candles overlooked by a statue of the Virgin Mary. Lighting a candle for Paola, she prayed for health, love, and happiness for her daughter.

Feeling miserable, she sat down to think in a side chapel. She tried to reassure herself she was doing the right thing. It was best for Paola. It would be simpler this way, and would bring so much happiness to Maria. And maybe even for her, in the long term. She just wished Sergio could grow to truly love her, and somehow find it within himself to show her.

She gave herself a mental shake: she needed to stop the self-pity. She'd agreed to get married on Saturday, so just had to pull herself together and get on with it.

* * *

On the way back to the house, Sergio asked whether Iris would like to stop off somewhere for lunch, or go to the shops to pick up anything she might need for the wedding. She frostily declined: not only did she not want to spend any more time than she absolutely had to alone with

Sergio, but she was feeling very insecure and wanted to be with Paola.

Arriving at the villa, Iris immediately found herself dragged into a frenzy of wedding preparations: Maria had the kitchen table covered with fabrics, pieces of paper, and flowers, all of which Iris and Sergio needed to make immediate decisions on. Sergio translated Maria's playful, "You can only blame yourselves for insisting upon getting married so quickly!" Iris smiled hollowly in reply. Maria really did seem to think that the swiftness of the wedding was purely down to their excitement at getting married at last. Maria was so happy; Iris knew she could never even hint all was not well between her and Sergio.

By the time Iris got into bed very late that night, the wedding was pretty much completely organised. Sergio and Carmen, as well as Maria and her daughters, had called in a number of favours, and it looked like everything was going to be perfect for Saturday. Iris had to admit to herself that everyone had done an amazing job. The wedding would be beautiful. It was just a shame that the bride was dreading it, and would rather not be going at all.

Chapter 9

As the organ began piping out the beautiful, flowing tones of Pachelbel's Canon, Iris mused that this whole scenario would look so perfect to an outsider. The day had dawned bright and blue-skied, the coolness of the old building making a welcome respite from the warm sun. The traditional stone church was full of gorgeous flowers and happy people, all done up in their finest clothes, thrilled to be witnessing such a joyous occasion. It was any bride's dream.

Iris stood alone in the vestibule. Her mother, unsurprisingly, had declined to come, so she had no family here to give her away, and felt the symbolism of making this last walk by herself. She felt honoured to be wearing Maria's wedding dress — it had been tailored to fit her perfectly, and it was so touching that Maria wanted her to use it. Yet, Iris felt terribly guilty as she readied herself to walk down the aisle. Sergio's mother thought this was a day for jubilation: she believed Iris and her son would live happily ever after. It would break Maria's heart if she knew the truth. In fact, Iris realised her own heart was very close to breaking. She should be so happy, marrying the father of her beautiful daughter. A man that under different circumstances she'd be absolutely thrilled to be walking down the aisle towards. But despite all her reasoning, all her rational weighing of the advantages, and despite her love for Sergio, she couldn't help worrying that making her marriage vows in this way was horribly, horribly wrong.

Sergio wasn't helping. What she needed was some reassurance, to be told that everything would be alright, that they were doing the right thing, and that he appreciated her. What she got was demands, instructions and, the final insult, a prenup to sign. After all she'd done, and all she was preparing to do, to be presented with that the night before their wedding was just typical of how insensitive he could be. Hurt and insulted, she hadn't even bothered to read the document, just signed it and wordlessly handed it back to him.

Iris's feet felt heavy as she forced them, one in front of the other, down the aisle. Staring straight in front of her, she willed the ceremony to be already over. She couldn't let her eyes deviate lest they accidentally met Maria's and her composure failed her. Seeing Paola might also be disastrous — despite the fact that Iris knew she was largely going through with the marriage for her, she felt that she'd let her child down in a way: marrying Sergio, like this, was giving in, an admission of sorts that by herself she hadn't and couldn't provide for all Paola needs.

Curiously, her veil definitely helped, obscuring the scene and adding a dreamlike quality, making her feel detached. Before she knew it, she found herself standing alongside Sergio. As he lifted up the veil, Iris lowered her eyes, looking anywhere but his face.

She was barely aware of what Father Garcia said, and if she had tried to follow his thick Catalan, she would only have been able to grasp snatches of it anyway. Tense, nervous, and overwhelmed, she really didn't know what she thought anymore. She loved Sergio, and becoming a family with him and Paola should have made her so happy. But getting married like this . . . it just didn't feel right.

Hearing the priest say her name, Iris was drawn back and forced herself to meet Sergio's searching eyes. They held each other's gaze. He opened his mouth to say something to her, but shook his head as if changing his mind. Instead he suddenly turned to Father Garcia and began speaking very rapidly in Catalan. The priest replied, clearly shocked, and Sergio turned his attention back to Iris. He appeared unsettled and unhappy.

Taking her hands in his, Sergio searched her face. "I cannot do this, preciosa," he said quietly. Stunned, she stood frozen. He kissed her tenderly on the forehead and walked solemnly out of the church.

The instant he went through the large wooden doors and disappeared from view, the spell was broken and a low murmur began to rise throughout the nave. Everyone turned to stare at Iris and see what her reaction would be. Bewildered, unsure what to do, she remained rooted to the spot, but seconds later found herself surrounded by Sergio's mother and sisters. They formed a protective wall around her, leading her back down the aisle, whispering what she assumed were words of support. Someone passed Paola to her, and she was hurried into the car which had been waiting outside to take her and Sergio to their reception. She looked around as they drove off, but there was no sign of Sergio.

Chapter 10

Feeling completely humiliated, Iris left Spain. Back at the villa, she'd called a cab and thrown as many of her and Paola's things as she could find into a bag. Sergio wasn't around, and even if had been, he surely wouldn't object to her returning to England now. She'd tearfully kissed Maria goodbye, hating to leave so abruptly. Maria seemed as upset and confused as she was, but Iris hadn't felt there was anything else she could do. She certainly wasn't going to wait around for Sergio to turn up.

She was extremely grateful that her very tired and confused little girl fell fast asleep as soon as the plane took off. It gave her some time to think. She sank down into her seat, her cheeks involuntarily going bright red, remembering the moment when Sergio had walked out of the church. She was glad she hadn't had to face him afterwards and felt as if any bond they'd ever had, was finally broken. It was over.

Spinning round and round in her head was one huge question: what had happened? She'd done, or rather tried to do, what he'd wanted. She'd even signed his prenup without making a fuss. He'd certainly appeared to have no doubts about going through with the marriage, so why did he change his mind at the last minute? Did he feel so little for her that in the end he couldn't bring himself to marry her, even for Paola's sake? She didn't have the answers. Exhausted and on autopilot, she just wanted to get to her flat, a place that might no longer feel like home, but which at least was hers.

However, once she was back, standing in her tiny, cold sitting room, Iris found she didn't experience the relief she'd been so sure she'd find there. She longed for that busy, happy villa, filled with people and laughter.

* * *

She and Paola had been in England for just under a week. The little girl looked paler in the grey London light, quieter, and less inclined to smile quite so readily. She asked about her father very frequently.

Iris hadn't seen Sergio since she'd flown back from Spain, though he called daily to speak to his daughter. She'd put Paola on the phone, but made it plain she herself had nothing to discuss with him. What was there to say?

She felt exhausted, sick, and lethargic. She wanted to pretend it was because of the cold English weather, and nothing to do with the deep sadness running through her. But no matter the anger, the shame, or how she wished otherwise, she missed Sergio with all her heart. And unfortunately, with a feeling of déjà vu, she knew her melancholy didn't explain everything. A great part of her malaise was due to something very different, something that was going to make her relations with Sergio even more complicated, and which she really wasn't ready to deal with just yet.

* * *

She stared out of the window at the overcast evening sky and damp, dirty buildings. It was only seven thirty, but dusk already enveloped everything. The weather was supposed to worsen overnight, and she didn't relish the thought of getting up early the next morning to take Paola to playgroup. The brightness and light of Spain seemed a world away.

Like the weather outside, she had to admit that her life in England lacked colour — except for when Paola was with her, she thought with a smile. But Paola would be at school full-time in just a couple of years, and probably staying with Sergio for at least part of the holidays. Iris reflected sadly that her little girl really was the only good thing in her life.

Lonely, with Paola in bed, and generally tired and nauseous, she forced herself to focus on the computer screen. She needed to concentrate on her work though she was ready for bed herself. She was glad she'd decided to turn down the promotion, especially now. Maybe when Paola was older she'd consider taking on additional work, but right now she knew Paola having her mummy around was far more important than extra money.

She'd been doing nothing but thinking: evaluating her priorities, wants, and needs; what she was doing and where she was going. Over the past months she'd often been so determined to disagree with Sergio that she hadn't bothered to listen to the sense in what he'd said about her life. Rather than being against her, she saw that he knew her better than she knew herself. And had, in his bullish, domineering way, been doing all he could to make her happy.

Could she say the same thing about herself? Had she really tried to make him happy? She'd agreed to marry him, but in her hurt had pushed him away and done her best to punish him. He'd been so forgiving of her mistakes, as unforgivable as they were. What forgiveness had she shown him?

"Was it my fault?" she said out loud. Sergio may have left her at the altar, but she couldn't really blame him, could she? It wasn't like she'd ever told him how she felt. It had always been him trying to bring them together. She never should have let anything come between her and the father of her child, especially not her silly pride and temper. He'd wanted to marry her, and spend the rest of his life with her. Why hadn't she just been happy and grateful for what she had, instead of wallowing in her self-sacrifice and complaining about the way he'd handled things? Maybe then, he would have happily married her, and eventually grown to love her as she did him.

Feeling particularly queasy as she contemplated her future without Sergio by her side, she reminded herself that there had been no guarantee his affection for her would have blossomed, and what sort of marriage would they have had with the love being so one-sided.

As it was, they'd simply have to find a way to get along for Paola's sake at least. Sergio would soon be returning to the UK for a fortnight. They hadn't talked about where he'd live long-term, but Iris assumed he'd still spend a lot of his time in London. Despite what had happened between them, he was determined to play a large part in Paola's life.

She really didn't know how she could face him. It was hard enough when he called to speak to Paola.

Getting up to make herself some supper, she couldn't help but notice how shabby her flat was. She'd become used to rather more luxurious settings. She quickly admonished herself — her place might be small and not as nice as Sergio's or Maria's, but when she'd found out she was pregnant, she'd made sure that she provided her baby with a warm, loving home. Paid for herself. She was proud she'd managed on her own. Plus, as she was always telling Sergio, money wasn't everything: love and family were far more important.

She was so caught up in her thoughts that she almost didn't hear the first knock at the door. She wasn't expecting anyone, so ignored it, suspecting it was just the local kids messing around again. When the second, louder knock came, curiosity got the better of her, and she went into the hall.

"Who's there?" she called out.

"It's me, Iris, I need to talk to you," came a strong, masculine voice she immediately recognised.

"What are you doing here, Sergio? I thought I made it quite clear on the phone that I didn't want to talk to you," she replied.

"Iris, please let me in," he said gently.

Knowing him, she was pretty sure he wouldn't leave without saying what he wanted to. She reluctantly opened the door, apprehensive yet struggling to contain her eagerness to see him. He was down on one knee, a ring in his hand.

"What are you doing?" she asked incredulously.

"I'm asking you to be my wife. The way I should have."

"Sergio, get up. People are staring."

"No. I'm here to ask you to forgive me, and to consider marrying me. Properly."

"There's no need for you to do this," she said. "You're here for Paola, I know. Don't worry: I'm not going to try to keep you from her, we've been through this, but I simply can't marry you."

"I'm not going to pressure you to marry me, Iris, I was very wrong to do that. That's why I left the church, I couldn't bear to see the look on your face — you were so unhappy. I should never have made you feel like that on our wedding day. It should have been one of the greatest days of your life," he said. "This isn't about Paola or what anyone else wants. I'm here because I love you. I want to be with you."

She turned away from him, trying to give herself a moment to get her emotions in check. She gestured for him to come inside. He did, closing the front door behind him, and followed her into the sitting room.

"How can I believe you?" she asked, finally.

"How can you not believe me? How can you not see the love in my eyes? I've loved you since we first met outside my office. My feelings have only grown stronger since I found you again. Iris, I adore our daughter, you know that, but I'm very much in love with you. I want you both. I want a family."

"You can't always get what you want, Sergio, we're not a business deal."

"I know, and I've done many things very wrong. I want the chance to make amends."

"Maybe you don't deserve that chance."

"Perhaps not, but we do, Iris."

She was silent, not trusting herself to speak lest she betray the torrent of emotion building up within her.

"I may not always do everything right, Iris, but I've only ever wanted you to be happy. You mean everything to me."

"But you only proposed to me because of your mother," she said, finding her voice.

"What makes you think that?"

"You didn't deny it when I asked you on the night of your mother's party!"

"I knew our marriage would please her, but she's not the reason I asked you. Surely my actions must have shown you that, even if my words were not right! I asked you to marry me because I wanted to spend the rest of my life with you."

"You couldn't have been too sure of that when you got me to sign a prenup!"

"But then you didn't read it! I only had it drawn up for you, to make you secure. So you knew that whatever happened between us, you and Paola would always have money, and you would have custody of her. I was trying to show you I had your interests at heart, not just my own."

"No, I didn't read it," Iris admitted, her stomach sinking. "I was too angry with you, and I thought it was to ensure I didn't get your money if we divorced."

"Iris," he said, taking her hands in his own, "that's honestly not what it was about. I wanted you to have security and independence."

"I've been really stupid, haven't I?" she said quietly.

"Maybe," he replied with a cautious smile. "But so have I."

"Can you forgive me?"

"If you can also forgive me, preciosa."

Iris nodded and Sergio took her in his arms and showered in kisses

Eventually she pulled away and asked, "So, do you still want to marry me?"

"Whenever you like, my darling."

"I think we should have the wedding as soon as possible, in Spain with all your family!"

"And you call me impatient!"

"I want to be your wife and get settled in our home together before Paola's little brother or sister makes an appearance," she said with a shy smile.

His eyes widened with a mixture of surprise and delight.

"Are you really . . .?" Sergio's grin somehow managed to grow even wider.

"Yes."

"But we—"

"—were clearly not careful enough!" she said, finishing his sentence with a laugh. She cautiously added, "Are you pleased?"

"Of course I am pleased, preciosa. I am more than pleased! I'm ecstatic!"

He was about to sweep Iris up in his arms, but was stopped by a small hand pulling on the leg of his trousers. He bent down and picked Paola up.

"Papa!" said the little girl happily. "You're here!"

"I missed you both too much to stay away any longer. What are you doing up, my darling?"

"I heard you," Paola replied, "You look all smiley, Mama!"

"That's because I feel all smiley, sweetheart," Iris said, as she joined her daughter and Sergio in what they would always remember as their first real hug as a real family.

THE END

If you enjoyed this book please leave feedback on Amazon, and if there is anything we missed or you have a question about then please get in touch. Thanks for taking the time to read this book.
Our email is jasper@joffebooks.com

www.joffebooks.com

ABOUT THE AUTHOR

Emma lives in Wales with her husband in a house full of children and animals. For more about Emma please visit her website: www.emma-bennet.co.uk

Also available by Emma Bennet

THE GREEN HILLS OF HOME

A delightful romance that you won't be able to put down

Gwen Jones has just signed her first book deal. She really needs it to work out so she can save her family home and look after her sick mother. But there's a big problem. She's falling in love with her handsome but arrogant editor, John Thatcher, and he's got a few secrets up his sleeve.

Can Gwen save her beautiful Welsh farmhouse home? And will she ever be able to tell John her real feelings?

Printed in Great Britain
by Amazon.co.uk, Ltd.,
Marston Gate.